**WHAT KIND OF C[OP]
SUSPECTED CRIM[INALS UP]
MULHOLLAND DR[IVE]
ABOVE LOS ANGELES AND D[RIVE]
THEM OFF A CLIFF?**

What kind of cop would bust into a child molester's private party and OD him with the heroin that he was about to shoot up his latest Lolita with?

What kind of cop would cheat on his wife with a beautiful woman who was every man's dream of sexual heaven and who made that dream come true with one man too many?

The cop's name is Hoover, and he leads a unit of three other cops into a realm beyond the law where justice is dispensed by a jury of four with no argument from the defence and no hope of appeal.

MULHOLLAND FALLS

A Novel
by Robert Tine

Based on the Story by
Pete Dexter and Floyd Mutrux
and the Screenplay
by Pete Dexter

A SIGNET BOOK

SIGNET

Published by the Penguin Group
Penguin Books Ltd, 27 Wrights Lane, London W8 5TZ, England
Penguin Books USA Inc., 375 Hudson Street, New York, New York 10014, USA
Penguin Books Australia Ltd, Ringwood, Victoria, Australia
Penguin Books Canada Ltd, 10 Alcorn Avenue, Toronto, Ontario, Canada M4V 3B2
Penguin Books (NZ) Ltd, 182–190 Wairau Road, Auckland 10, New Zealand

Penguin Books Ltd, Registered Offices: Harmondsworth, Middlesex, England

First published in the USA in Signet 1996
First published in Great Britain in Signet 1996
1 3 5 7 9 10 8 6 4 2

Film and TV Tie-in edition

Printed in England by Clays Ltd, St Ives plc

MULHOLLAND
FALLS

PROLOGUE

Pastel green, top down—a '51 Chevy driven fast and straight by a beautiful woman on a desert road: Allison Pond knew she looked good. She was a heart-stopping, reckless beauty with eyes the color of jade stone and a cupid's bow mouth, the red of her lips contrasting with the creamy whiteness of her soft skin and her long hair, black like midnight.

There was something about her, a faint whiff of brimstone perhaps or that slightly wicked cast to her smile, that suggested danger. Perhaps her desire burned a little too hot or her craving for freedom came a little too close to frenzy.

Allison had a soft voice with an overlay of Los Angeles sophistication, but somewhere beneath that there was a different note, a piece of flint wrapped in velvet, the smooth huskiness of the backwoods or the Badlands—Oklahoma, maybe, or the Texas panhandle. It was the kind of voice that could cheer up her man, put him back on his feet, and make him feel ten feet tall or cuss him out like some hard-as-whip-leather hillbilly Marine Corps DI on Parris Island.

She could do the kind of things men liked. She drove like a man, she could drink like a man, in bed she pleased the way men like to be pleased.

One arm resting on the hot metal of the door, the steering wheel loose under her elegant right hand, Allison kept the car at top speed. Patti Page sang "Detour" on the radio but the Chevrolet was streaking across the desert, the chrome-encrusted nose pointed toward Las Vegas. Allison had that look on her face that hinted she was on her way to see her lover.

The casino, the Double Diamond, sat on a piece of raw desert on the northern edge of Las Vegas. There was no point in being downtown—there was no downtown, not yet, anyway—just a widening in the road and a few flyblown stores stocking things that out of towners didn't need or want. The casinos were being built out here, on the edge of the newborn city, places where hotels would go up and where golf courses would be built and irrigated with mob money.

In 1953 Las Vegas was still a new town, a place in the desert where someone had built a couple of dozen casinos and bars. There were a couple of gas stations, a couple of wedding chapels, and a working class housed in trailers.

There had been gambling in Las Vegas since the thirties, but it was desultory, unorganized, and left largely to a handful of roadside honkytonks and bars, where crooked slot machines were merely implements for fleecing a few nickels out of Okies, hicks, and servicemen making their way across the country. Gambling was not nearly as profitable as it could have—should have—been.

The first hotels were not profitable at all.

Sure, Raymond Smith was doing okay with Harold's Club, up in Reno, but it was too far from where the nearest high rollers lived—the movie people and would-be movie people—in Los Angeles to take in the real dough. Las Vegas was where the action was going to be. But it took awhile—and it took the mob.

Bugsy Siegel—his friends called him Ben— had been murdered by those friends who called him Ben because the hotel he built, the Flamingo, cost a lot of his friends money and made back very little.

But by the early fifties the casinos were catching on. They had followed the murdered Bugsy

Siegel's initial instincts and had begun to offer more than just a chance to lose all your money. The gaming houses were hiring entertainment—mostly singers and comics, some magic acts, once in a while a jazz band. But this was Nevada in the early fifties—how good could a jazz band be if there were no blacks allowed? The casinos would be lily-white for years to come.

Allison's car skidded to a stop on the gravel drive at the Double Diamond front door. A valet in one of those "Paging Philip Morris" monkey suits opened the door of the car, his eyes sweeping over Allison's curves. He could not stop himself gazing at her as she crossed the driveway, her red mules crunching the gravel, her body swaying as she walked, as if she was moving to some music deep inside her that only she could hear.

She walked through the cool lobby and out onto the patio at the rear of the hotel. There was a bar out there, a wide expanse of flagstone sheltered from the sun by a huge white canvas canopy.

Even though it was coming up on three o'clock in the afternoon, the place was full. A piano player in a white suit was playing a white baby grand, people were laughing and feeling naughty at getting looped on a Tuesday afternoon when the rest of the world was at work. Everybody in the place was drinking, and just about everyone had on a pair of sunglasses, and if anyone had bothered to notice, every chair in the bar was facing north. The mood was festive, more like a party on an ocean liner than a bunch of strangers drinking in a casino bar.

A cocktail waitress was delivering an eye-opener, a Bloody Mary, to a young man, his face obscured by the heavy 16 millimeter Bolex movie camera he held to his eye, he panned the area, the lens coming to rest on Allison. As she crossed the bar—every eye in the place following her—she winked at the camera and then mugged a little, tilting her head and pouting, at once glamorous and self-mocking.

As if to see her better, he put down the camera, and without taking his eyes off her, he reached for his drink and sipped. He was a slim, almost too beautiful young man—the kind of man Allison could really flip for if he were richer and liked women in the first place.

Nonetheless, she was here to meet him. They kissed each other lightly on the cheek.

"Jimmy . . ." she murmured.

"So here we are," Jimmy Fields said, "Chuck and Bambi from Reno. And Chuck and Bambi are on their honeymoon—okay, lovely, great."

Allison picked up the camera and, mocking

him, filmed him looking petulant until he laughed in spite of himself. She put down the camera and laughed with him.

"Bambi has very good taste . . . 'cause Chuck is very cute," Allison said as she slid into the chair next to him.

"Isn't he though," said Jimmy as he signaled for the waitress. "A gin and tonic for the lady, please."

Abruptly, the piano player stopped playing and pulled the microphone from its stand.

"Well, folks, it's three o'clock on the first day of June. The temperature outside in downtown Las Vegas is 110 degrees, the wind is four miles an hour from the northeast." He paused a moment as a gust of reverb shimmered through the air. "The weatherman says the cloud will pass west of the city . . . out by the Spring of Youth Trailer Park, so a big hello to all you trailer dwellers who came into town with the rest of us to enjoy the show . . ."

The waitress put an icy gin and tonic down in front of Allison.

"The show begins in two minutes," announced the piano player, glancing at his watch. "Two minutes from now."

The few people not wearing dark glasses put them on, and everyone looked to the northern horizon.

Jimmy Fields sighed and shrugged. "I mean, how many of these things can you watch?"

Allison Pond sipped her drink and smiled teasingly at Fields. "I like them," she said, as if her wish should be enough to explain anything.

"Okay," said Jimmy, "but why do you have to drag me along?"

"Because you're my friend," she said.

Jimmy Fields gave her a tight smile, but it was plain that he resented the consequences of being Allison's friend while at the same time acknowledging its claim. Allison patted him on the back of the hand.

"My very best friend," she said, slipping on her own glasses and looking to the horizon. The crowd stirred, a rustle of anticipation. Jimmy aimed his camera to the north.

In that moment a huge but eerily silent flash lit up the sky—a white light as hard and as harsh as a flashbulb multiplied by the millions. A few seconds of utter stillness, of absolute quiet, then a rumbling came across the desert like a storm, the roar doubling and redoubling, building on itself until the sound was huge. A moment later a dry hot wind followed it across the desert, the rush of air pressing Allison's blouse against her skin, blowing napkins off the tables, rattling the glasses. The canopy billowed and snapped like a giant sail.

To the north, a mushroom cloud slowly rose from the charred earth. It was huge and terrifying, but beautifully colored by the sun and the dust within it. Allison Pond could not take her eyes from it, and her lips were parted and her body was tense, as if she could feel the power of the blast within her.

1

"Doctor, doctor," said the comic. "It hurts when I go like that. The doctor says, don't go like that."

The nightclubbers laughed or groaned or, like Allison Pond, paid no attention at all.

The comic tapped the mike. "Hey, is this thing on?"

The lighting in the room was low and the walls were lined with red plush, but even in the gloom Allison's beauty seemed to shine. The café lamp on her table was gold and warm, and it caught her eyes and seemed to make them glow like a cat's. She sat at a table near the stage; there were three men with her, and every other man in the room envied one of them.

From the look of things, the man to resent

was Jimmy Fields. He and Allison sat side by side, as if they were a couple. Across the table were two men, older and more distinguished-looking than young Jimmy.

One was dressed in the gray uniform of a bird colonel. He wore a disapproving look on his face. The other man, older, the colonel's boss, was dressed like Jimmy in a dark dinner suit. He could not stop looking at Allison, and from time to time his hand touched her bare back.

"I tell ya," said the comic, "Vegas is a tough town. Most of the places, the hatcheck girl is named Dominic."

Colonel Fitzgerald sat stiff and still, uninterested in the act onstage, staring with poorly disguised contempt at Jimmy Fields. Allison saw it and didn't like it. She raised her glass and toasted the older man.

"To you, General Timms. To your job, your desert. To your beautiful explosions . . ." She smirked at Colonel Fitzgerald. "You're missing the show, Colonel."

"I don't have no luck, really," said the comic. "I bought a used car, my wife's dress is on the backseat."

Fitzgerald sighed. "I've seen the show, Miss Pond," he said wearily. "I've seen it many, many times . . ."

Jimmy Fields thought this was funny—funnier than the comic, anyway. He laughed heartily.

"Colonel, please . . ." said Timms in mild reprimand.

"Sorry, sir," said the colonel. He thought: *there's no fool like an old fool who's just discovered sex*.

"I get in a cab," said the comic. "I tell the driver to take me where the action is. He takes me to *my* place."

The floor manager appeared and whispered something in Fitzgerald's ear. The colonel, in turn, whispered something to General Timms. Both men stood up.

"Would you excuse us a moment," the general asked.

"Of course," said Allison.

Jimmy and Allison watched the two men leave. The moment they were out of sight, Allison sighed heavily and seemed to relax.

"You really think he's going to divorce his wife and marry you?" Jimmy asked quietly.

"And you don't," Allison responded.

"Look, he's the chairman of the Atomic Energy something or other."

"Commission," said Allison.

"He's a general. And he must be at least fifty years old," said Jimmy derisively. From the vantage point of his early twenties, courtly General Timms seemed as old as Eisenhower.

"He's forty-eight," said Allison. "That's not so old." She looked sharply at Jimmy. "Anyway, that's not what matters, you know . . ."

"Really? What matters then?" Jimmy leaned forward, smiling a cynical smile that did not sit well on his pretty-boy features.

"Maybe I love him."

"Remember what happened when you loved the other guy?" If he was trying to hurt her, he succeeded. She winced once, as if he had found a bruise and pressed hard on it. Jimmy grabbed her wrists, but Allison pulled away quickly, hitting him on the hand as she did so.

"Never mind that," she said pointedly. "He's not like that. This one is good to me."

"And you're good to him . . ." Fields countered.

Allison nodded. "That's right. I'm good for him."

Jimmy Fields put his hand to his brow and pantomimed thinking hard. "Hmmmmm, seems to me there's a word for that. Begins with a p. Pro? Pros? Something . . ."

"Is that what you think?" Allison asked.

"I think he likes fucking you, Allison, and fucking doesn't last. We both know that, don't we?"

Timms and Fitzgerald returned to the table, but did not sit down. It was plain that Fitzgerald was making no attempt to hide his contempt for Jimmy and Allison. It was obvious to both men that they had been having some kind of tiff.

"Is everything all right?" Timms asked.

"Things are fine, General," said Allison. "Are you leaving us?"

Fitzgerald looked at Timms, as if Allison's question proved some point he had been making. The general only smiled at his adjutant's rectitude.

"Unfortunately. We have to get back right away," said Timms. "Suddenly, we have a very early morning at the test site."

Abruptly, Allison stood. "I'll come with you," she announced. "That is, if you don't mind . . ."

"Mind? No," said General Timms, "I don't mind in the least."

Colonel Fitzgerald looked at both of them as if they had suddenly taken leave of their senses. "Sir," he said, "she has no clearance to be out there. The regulations are very specific on that."

Timms ignored his aide-de-camp. It was as if he wasn't even in the room. "It's all desert out there, Allison," he said. "There's not much to look at."

She smiled softly and caught his eyes with hers. "Then, I'll look at you," she said with a shrug.

"I go to the doctor, and he tells me I've got three months to live," the comic brayed. "I said I'd like a second opinion. He says, okay, you're ugly, too."

2

Six thousand pounds of Buick Roadmaster rolled to a halt in front of Frankie's Grill, a restaurant on Sunset Boulevard. The car was jet-black with red upholstery and filling the seats, front and back, were four very big men in suits and hats. Taken together they added another twelve hundred pounds to the weight of the car.

A valet scrambled to open the door.

"Don't park it," ordered the driver. "Keep it right here."

"But there's no parking on Sunset, sir."

"Don't worry about it," the big man growled.

The valet was not going to worry about it. The four men, particularly this one, who seemed to be the leader, conveyed not only massiveness, but also an implacable menace.

As the men moved toward the double doors of the restaurant, they separated—three of them went through the front door, but the fourth went down the side alley, looking for a back door.

There was a goon just inside the door, his arms folded across his chest, blocking the way.

"Who the hell are you?" he asked.

"I'm Eddie Hall," said one of the men. And without breaking stride, Hall jammed the heel of his hand into the thug's forehead, snapping the man's head back against the door frame. The gangster went down like old timber, a heap of flashy suit on the carpeted floor. The other two men hardly glanced at this sudden and vicious display of violence. They had seen Eddie Hall work before.

Frankie's Grill was a mobbed-up restaurant that drew Hollywood types. The men were beefy but well dressed—except for the jewelry that some of them sported. The women were curvaceous, young, expensive, and they had a penchant for jewelry as well. The atmosphere seemed to pulsate with a faint, thrilling air of criminality, as well as a heavy dose of sex.

The three men looked straight ahead, ignoring a maître d' who was bustling over to intercept them. The kitchen door pushed open, and the fourth member of the team emerged.

"Anyone out back, Relyea?" the leader asked.

"One. I took care of him," Relyea replied. He was the youngest member of the group, and the most handsome.

In the far corner of the room, at the prime corner booth in an alcove was a group of men— men drinking too much and laughing too loud. These were big guys, too, tough-looking, and the bulges under their jackets were not flab but hardware.

The noisiest of the men, Jack Flynn was a stocky, fair-haired man who seemed to have a ring on every finger. He was roaring with laughter as he peeled a wet ten-dollar bill off the table and slapped it on the forehead of the man sitting next to him. The laughter got louder.

The man with the bill on his forehead did not look like the other men. He was smaller, better-looking, with the fine features and the anointed bearing of a movie star—which is what he was. He was used to being the center of attention, but in the crowd of made men, he was nothing more than a court jester. He peeled the bill off his forehead and handed it to a cigarette girl who rolled it up and tucked it between her breasts.

The men from the Buick entered the alcove;

the driver, Maxwell Hoover, leading the way. Hoover was in his forties, but breathing hard on fifty, an aging lion who could still show determination and a distinct capacity for violence—in this setting at least. He was a cop—they were all cops'—and the unquestioned leader of the group.

Behind him was Eddie Hall. He was younger than Hoover by five years or so. He was good-looking in a tough, broken-nosed way. Hall was a ladies' man, even in a situation like this—he had already scoped out the cigarette girl, shooting her a wink and getting a coy smile in return.

Ellery Coolidge and Arthur Relyea walked in side by side. Coolidge was taller than the others, but his bruiser looks did not betray his amiable nature. He was naturally friendly, and he knew he talked too much.

The men around Ryan and the movie star had seen the four men now, and the laughter had stopped. One of the men at the table stood with an "I'll take care of this" air, reaching inside his sharp sharkskin jacket for his nickel-plated automatic. As he pulled the weapon from the holster, Relyea was on him. One beefy forearm snaked around the tough's throat in a choke hold, the left hand closing around the gun hand.

Relyea pinned the hoodlum with little effort, his hand squeezing hard on the gun, crushing his fingers against the ungiving metal of the weapon. The mobster's eyes widened in pain as his figners cracked like kindling. Relyea dropped the man in a heap and then knocked him out with a sharp blow to the chin.

Jack Flynn had not moved except to put a cigarette in his mouth. He smiled around the butt, sort of enjoying this experience.

Max Hoover leaned over the table. "Jack Flynn?" His voice was only slightly louder than a whisper.

Flynn flipped a twenty-dollar bill at Hoover. "Here you go, pal," said Flynn. "Go buy yourself a good time." He followed up his actions with a forced laugh, looking to his goombahs for support. But they didn't laugh, not this time.

"Hey," said Flynn. "You still here?"

"My name is Maxwell Hoover," he said patiently. "I am with the Los Angeles Police Department . . ."

"Hey," said Flynn jovially. "This means I must be getting some change back from that twenty."

A couple of the hoodlums dared a laugh this time.

But Maxwell Hoover was unruffled. "I came here to deliver a message, Mr. Flynn."

"You did, huh? What message?"

"Your presence is required back in Chicago," said Hoover evenly. "Do you understand?"

"It's cold in Chicago," said Flynn with a laugh. "That's why I moved here. Nice weather."

"You should buy a coat," said Hoover.

Flynn shrugged and threw up his hands. "What's this all about? I'm trying to eat here."

The movie star spoke up. "Is Mr. Flynn being charged with a crime?" he asked. "Has he done something illegal."

Hoover looked at him as if he was a monkey who had suddenly started speaking the king's English. "Are you a lawyer?"

The movie star shook his head. "No," he said. "But I'm represented by a very good one. Now, what's Mr. Flynn being charged with?"

"He did things in Chicago," said Hoover.

"I beat all that," said Flynn. "I beat those indictments." Flynn was speaking seriously for the first time now.

Then everything seemed to happen fast. Eddie Hall grabbed Flynn by a lapel and yanked him to his feet. The tough next to the movie star started to reach for his weapon, but Hall used his free hand to slam the man's face into his plate, smashing both his face and his dish. Hall kept his hand on the back of the bruiser's head, mashing his face deeper into the food.

Now Flynn looked worried. The other goons were tense, poised to intervene, but one look at Relyea, Hall, and Coolidge kept them in their places. The movie star stood up, but suddenly realized he wasn't a tough guy himself, that any screen toughness he projected was make-believe made by the careful use of makeup and close-up. But this was Hollywood, and he was a movie star and Hoover was just a cheap cop.

"You don't know who I am ?"

"Anybody know who this guy is?" Hoover called over his shoulder.

Coolidge studied the movie star's fine features for a moment, then he turned to Hoover. "He used to be an actor, didn't he? He used to be . . . Lance—Lance something."

Way in the back of his mind, Relyea heard a faint bell. "Hey," the young man said. "You played the sergeant in Battle Cry, didn't you?"

The movie star nodded. It was an unnerving feeling for a movie star to go unrecognized.

"Oh, yeah," said Hall. "I remember him now." Hall grinned. "You better be careful, Max. Lance something here has played a lot of tough guys. Maybe he *thinks* he's a tough guy."

The movie star put a cigar in his mouth, chuckling as he did so. "The LAPD," he said, shaking his head. "God help us . . ."

Very slowly, Hoover said: "If I were you,

Lance, I'd sit down." Then Hoover swung his big hand and slapped the cigar out of Lance's mouth, the force of the blow so great that it knocked him into his chair, and the chair went tumbling over backward.

Hoover pointed to Flynn. "Get him out of here."

Hall laughed and lifted the head of the man he had been mashing into his food. "Bye now," he said.

As they walked Jack Flynn out the door, Coolidge grabbed a plate of fettucine with clam sauce.

"Looks good," he said. Coolidge had a weakness for food. Any kind of food.

3

The big Buick didn't break a sweat as it climbed through the Hollywood Hills, winding up through the dark bluffs, the headlights stabbing forward into the night. The top was up, and the four cops were in their usual places. Max Hoover was at the wheel, Eddie Hall in the passenger seat beside him, Ellery Coolidge and Relyea in the backseat.

Jack Flynn was in the middle of the backseat, squashed between the considerable bulk of Relyea and Coolidge. Dwarfed by these men so much bigger than he, Flynn felt a hot core of apprehension somewhere deep in his belly. The interior of the car was redolent with the pungent smell of garlic rising from the plate of fettucine and clams that Coolidge was just finishing up.

The odor of the food mixed with the sour scent of Flynn's fear made him queasy, and he had to fight to keep his gorge down.

Eddie Hall turned, resting a muscular arm across the backseat, and looked at Flynn with great curiosity, as if examining a peculiar specimen in a museum of natural history.

"Where are we going?" Flynn asked.

"The airport," Hall answered. "You're going to the airport, Jack. You got to get back to Chicago as soon as possible."

Flynn shot a look out the window. He may have been new to Los Angeles, but he knew his way around. "This ain't the way to the airport," he said. "What is it with you guys?"

Hoover looked at Flynn in the rearview mirror. "It's a shortcut, Jack," he said. "Remember to tell your friends about it."

Eddie Hall gave Flynn a reassuring pat on the knee, then turned back to watch the road.

Flynn's brow furrowed. "My friends . . . ? What are you going to do? What's this all about?"

The Buick had reached the summit of the hill, the city spread out beneath, a carpet of lights from the hills to the dark of the sea. They were on Mulholland Drive, driving along the ridge crest now. Hoover slowed the car and pulled onto the shoulder, the fat whitewalls grinding up the gravel. He turned off the engine, but left the headlights on, the beams thrusting straight out into the open air like searchlights.

Hall turned in his seat again. "This is it," he said.

Ellery Coolidge looked mildly interested. "This is it?"

Relyea nodded. "Oh, yeah, this is it."

Flynn felt sick to his stomach. "This is what?" he demanded to know.

"This, Jack," said Eddie Hall, "is Mulholland Drive. And that"—he pointed to the precipice—"is Mulholland Falls."

Flynn shook his head, like a prizefighter shrugging off a blow, and his eyes narrowed. "Mulholland Falls?"

"Yeah," said Relyea, "you know, like Niagara Falls."

"Niagara Falls?" Flynn did his best to laugh. "There ain't no waterfalls in Los Angeles."

"Absolutely right, Jack," said Relyea. "No *water*falls . . ."

Flynn looked from Hall to Relyea. Now he was really terrified. This wasn't a shakedown, it was a hit. "You . . . You can't do this," he stammered. "This is America, for Christ's sake!"

Hoover opened the door of the car. "Wrong. This isn't America, Jack. This is L.A."

Relyea and Coolidge hustled Jack Flynn out of the car, each of them taking an arm and dragged him toward the crest of the hill.

Jack could guess what was going to happen next. "Hey, hey, hey, slow down," he said, panicked. "You guys—"

Without a word Relyea and Coolidge pushed Jack Flynn over the edge. The mobster hit the steep side and bounced, tumbling over the rocks and through the bushes and trees on the sharp incline.

The four cops peered down into the gloom, listening to Flynn scream and swear, his incoherent cries interrupted every time he hit something solid.

"I thought we weren't going to do this stuff anymore," said Coolidge. He tossed away his empty plate and belched silently.

The other three cops stared at him. "What? What stuff?" asked Hall.

"The throwing people down the side of a hill stuff," Coolidge replied. "You know?"

"Come on, Ellery," said Hoover. "Flynn was a scumbag who deserved a little rough treatment."

"Ellery," said Eddie Hall, speaking as if he was a kindly old uncle, "this therapy shit is messing up your head. It's making you way too sensitive."

"Way too sensitive," Hoover agreed.

Coolidge shrugged. "I don't know . . ." They all turned toward the car. "Maybe you're right . . ."

The Buick turned a corner at the bottom of the hill, the headlights catching the battered body of Jack Flynn sprawled on the side of the road like a piece of roadkill. Hoover stopped the car, and the four men gathered around Flynn. The mobster's eyes fluttered and opened, squinting into the glare of the headlights.

"Jack?" said Hoover.

Flynn hardly stirred. His face was scratched and bruised, blood oozing from a couple of deep gashes, and his hands were tattered and bloody, as if he was wearing a pair of gloves made from shredded skin. Jack Flynn's expensive suit was a mass of bedraggled rags.

"Maybe he's dead," said Eddie Hall matter-of-factly. Jack Flynn's mortality—or lack of it—didn't concern him all that much.

"He's not dead," said Ellery Coolidge. "Can't you tell, Eddie? He's looking right at us."

"I've seen stiffs with their eyes open," said Hall. "Happens all the time."

"Are you dead, Jack?" asked Hoover solicitously.

Jack Flynn moved slightly, as if trying to rouse himself from a deep sleep. He moaned and gingerly fingered the gash on his forehead. "Oh, God . . ." he said. "What happened?"

"You fell down," said Relyea.

"Hey!" said Eddie Hall, sounding genuinely pleased. "Jack's alive! What do you make of that!"

Hoover squatted down on his haunches and spoke slowly and clearly. "Can you hear me, Jack?" he said. "You don't have a stick in your ear do you? Sometimes that happens on the way down. You get something stuck in your ears."

Jack Flynn moaned again.

"I guess that means you can hear me . . ."

"Yeah," Flynn managed to gasp. "Yeah, I can hear you . . ." Flynn was doing his best to look Hoover in the eyes, but his vision was blurry and the images swam crazily in front of his eyes.

"That's good, Jack. Very good," said Hoover. "Now listen. We don't like people like you. We don't have organized crime in L.A. We don't want organized crime in L.A. So just look around and remember this all the way back to Chicago. Mulholland Falls, Jack. That's the name of the game."

A moment later the Buick sped away, showering Jack Flynn with gravel as the car peeled out.

4

The Paradise Ballroom was a dine and dance club just off Sunset, less showy than Jack Flynn's former hangout and with a clientele more to Max Hoover's liking. It was a tastefully plush room, refined but welcoming. There was a Meyer Davis-style band playing subdued arrangements of old standards from the decade before—"I Don't Care if the Sun Don't Shine," "On a Slow Boat to China," "For You, For Me, Forevermore"—it was 1953, Elvis Presley was a year away from recording his first record, and Maxwell Hoover was only dimly aware of something called rock'n'roll.

There were a number of couples dancing lazily to "You're Breaking My Heart" when Max Hoover entered the Paradise and a few of the tables were occupied with diners. There were two women at the bar, one of them, the attractive soft-featured blond, was Max's wife Katherine.

She looked pleased to see her husband. Hoover kissed his wife gently on the cheek. Away from the job, Hoover was a gentle-hearted, almost mild man. "Hi, Max," she said in her light, breathy, almost baby-doll voice. "You remember Lili."

"Sure, how are you, Lili?"

"We were just discussing husbands," said Katherine.

"Why, Kay?" Hoover asked. "Is there a shortage of them?"

Katherine nodded. "Yes there is. But only of good ones. I'm trying to find a new one for Lili. Know any?"

"Because I sure don't," said Lili with a rueful laugh.

Hoover signaled the bartender. He was known there, and he didn't have to do more than raise a finger to get his usual.

"Well, I'll tell you, Lili, I only know cops and bad guys. I'm not sure I'd recommend either one . . ." He sipped his drink and thought a moment. "How about Eddie Hall?"

Katherine laughed lightly. "Eddie Hall?"

"I like the name," said Lili. "Is he nice?"

"He's nice," said Hoover. "Nice, for a cop, that is."

"How many times has Eddie been married?" Katherine asked. "It's at least five times."

Hoover shrugged. "See what I mean?"

Lili had been single long enough to know exactly what point three became a crowd. She finished her drink and moved on, ignoring Katherine's polite entreaties that she stay.

When she left, Hoover moved in closer to his wife, his arm around her waist. "I'm sorry I was late, Kay. There was an accident up in the hills."

"That's okay," said Katherine. "Your hours are always irregular." Max sipped his drink, aware of his wife's eyes on him. He always wondered what she was thinking, if she could see on him the violence and sordidness that were the casual companions of his every working day.

The band was playing "Harbor Lights." Katherine was still smiling at him, looking radiant and swaying slightly to the beat of the music. Hoover smiled back, and then it dawned on him what she was up to.

"Oh, no, you don't, Kay . . . Come on, Kay, you know I'm no dancer. I've got flat feet."

But Katherine was not going to let her husband escape. She slid off her bar stool and led a very reluctant Max onto the dance floor. She maneuvered him into a cheek-to-cheek clinch and then began to lead him around the dance floor.

Katherine, no surprise, was graceful and light on her feet, Max was slower, a plodder, but she was happy that she had managed, at least, to coax him onto the floor. He always felt self-conscious on the dance floor, as if everyone in the place was watching him and sniggering behind their hands. It always took him some time to realize that, short of his breaking into a Mazurka or a Fandango, no one was paying the slightest bit of attention to him. So after a while, he relaxed and allowed himself to go with the flow, following the natural lead of the music.

"Max?" Katherine whispered in his ear.

Hoover pulled away a few inches to get a clearer view of her face, suddenly worried.

"I love you," said Katherine.

Hoover smiled and pulled her close again. She relaxed, happy and safe in his strong arms.

5

All four cops sat at the table playing cards; all four men were in their shirtsleeves, guns and suspenders exposed, but all four wore their fedoras. Around them the usual riot of a division police station was going on. Phones rang, cops hustled by late for their roll call, perps in the holding cells down the hall rattled the cages and shouted for their attorneys.

Hoover and his squad, though, were immune to the distractions. It was as if they projected some kind of aura, that the normal rules of policing did not apply to these four men. They went where they went when they wanted to go; they chose their cases. Their . . . unorthodox methods were known to some, but no matter how outrageous their exploits, there was never an official reprimand, not even so much as a slap on the wrists, a letter of censure in their files. Things were as quiet at their card table—and in their careers—as in the eye of a hurricane.

Three of them studied their cards while Coolidge put down his hand and turned himself to the task of carefully tucking the lettuce into his tuna fish sandwich. He was being compulsively neat about it, and it bothered the hell out of Eddie Hall, who kept on glancing at his cards, then over at the sandwich.

"Look at this guy," Hall grumbled. "He's making hospital corners with his lettuce."

"Like maybe some topkick sergeant is gonna come along and see if he can bounce a quarter on his sandwich," said Relyea. "You know, like in the service."

Coolidge did not look up from his meticulously executed task. "Shut up," he explained.

"I'm not criticizing the workings of the human mind, you understand," Hall continued. "But, Ellery, tell me—how can you buy a hamburger and put tuna fish on top of it?"

"It's very simple," said Coolidge. "It's my version of surf and turf. The burger, that's the turf. The fish, that's the surf. You want me to run that by you again there, Eddie, or did you get it the first time."

"Ellery," said Hall. "I speak as a friend . . . You need help."

"I'm getting help," said Coolidge. "Leave me alone."

Another brawny detective, older than Hoover's crowd, wandered over with a handful of telephone messages for the four detectives.

"Hey, Earl," said Hoover, looking up from his cards.

Earl studied Ellery Coolidge's towering sandwich for a moment. "You know, my Aunt Mabel, she used to get a steak and add butter . . . then she'd put a tomato on it and a nice little piece of pineapple on top. There you go . . ."

"I don't get it," said Relyea.

"Me, neither," said Hall.

"My Aunt Mabel would say that she was getting all four major food groups right there. You got your grain, your fruit, your meat, your dairy."

Relyea looked puzzled. "Where's the grain?"

"The tomato," said Earl. "That's the grain."

"Tomato isn't a grain," said Relyea.

"Yes it is," said Earl.

"No," Relyea insisted. "Wheat's a grain, barley's a grain. Rye . . ."

"Rye is booze," said Earl. "And bread."

"Anyway, tomato is not a grain," said Relyea. You should listen to him," said Eddie Hall.

"He's going to be a lawyer some day. Still hitting those books, Relyea?"

"Every chance I get, Eddie," said Relyea. "Every chance I get." Which, of course, meant not terribly often.

Earl started distributing his phone messages. "I still say tomato's a grain," the big cop grumbled.

"You know, Relyea," said Eddie, "when you become a lawyer, that means you joined the enemy."

"What if I become a prosecutor?" Relyea asked. "Won't we be on the same side then? Not that I give a damn . . ."

"If you become a prosecutor, that just means you're stupid," said Hall flatly. "I mean, why bother to become a shyster and then stay poor? That doesn't make any sense to me. Max, that make sense to you?"

Max Hoover was not listening. He had put down his cards to shuffle through his telephone messages. One of them had stopped him cold, and he was staring at it as if it was the death card. Scrawled on the scrap of paper were four words: Allison Pond—please call.

"Max?" said Relyea. "You still with us?"

"Yeah," said Hoover. He crumpled the phone message quickly, like a cheating man caught with a love letter and shot it into the ashtray on the table. He looked over at Relyea, who was staring at him curiously, as if he could sense that something had stirred the air in the room.

"What about the Abelson business, Relyea," said Hoover, sweeping away his cards and getting down to business. "You have something on that for me yet."

Relyea flipped open a wire-bound reporters' notebook. "We have the daughter is all," he said scanning his notes. "And we have the life insurance. But the lawyer told the kid not to talk to us . . ." Relyea shrugged. "So far, that's all we can get."

"She should talk to us," said Eddie Hall. "If she doesn't, we don't have a case on that one."

"No, it's not that," said Coolidge thoughtfully. "The lawyer is giving her the wrong advice. She needs to talk to us. She needs to get it out in the open. She needs to heal."

Eddie Hall looked disgusted. "Is that what that psychiatrist of yours told you, Ellery?"

Coolidge nodded. "Absolutely," he said emphatically. "Confession is more important than you think, Eddie."

"Like hell, I don't know that. How do you ever get a conviction without a confession?"

"You know what I mean," said Coolidge.

"Getting it out in the open was not your problem," said Eddie. "Right?"

Coolidge paused a moment, ignoring his colleague, then took another look at his monumental sandwich and took a nice, precise bite.

"I said, that wasn't your problem, right, Ellery?"

Hoover shot a sharp look at Hall. "Eddie," he said quietly. "You mind?"

"Sorry," Hall mumbled. Hoover's word was law.

Hoover's eyes dropped to the ashtray again, looking at the crumpled-up phone message. Allison Pond was a figure out of his past, a painful past that he had hoped he would never have to revisit.

He was deep in thought when the phone rang, and Earl had to call him twice before he heard him.

"Max," said Earl. "There's a bad one in the valley."

The first freeway in Los Angeles, the Arroyo Seco Parkway, was opened in 1940 and apart from the war years, Los Angeles had been building them ever since. These attenuated ribbons of concrete and asphalt were reaching farther and farther into the Los Angeles hinterland, extending to the groves and orchards of quiet farm towns dozens of miles from downtown. But there was more. At the end of these highways there was more building going on, housing subdivisions were being built, financed by men who seemed to divine the future.

There was no sizable population beyond the hills, but the building went on, great roads to serve a vast population of phantoms, foundations laid for houses yet to be bought. It was from the very end of one of these highways-in-the-making that the call came.

The Buick threw up a cloud of red dust as it rolled through the raw, torn earth of the excavation, Hoover maneuvering the car around huge pieces of construction equipment. The machines—colossal bulldozers and dump trucks, graders and backhoes—were there and many were running their engines on throaty idle, but there wasn't a soul around, as if the inanimate tools had come alive and had decided on their own to tackle this enormous undertaking.

The people were at the end of the line. The men of the work crews were standing around talking in the hushed tones that people always employ when they're talking about death.

A bulbous black-and-white '52 Studebaker Police Special stood at the head of the line of construction equipment like the grand marshal of a parade, the lights on the roof still winking blue to white to red.

A couple of cops and a man in overalls walked

toward Hoover and his crew, the cops looking a little self-important the way crime-scene cops always did, the guy in denims looking a little self-important the way the guy who discovers the body always does.

"You the foreman here?" Hall asked the workman.

"Yeah."

"What is this place?" Eddie asked.

"It's a new housing subdivision. We're building houses."

"Who for?" asked Coolidge.

The foreman shrugged. "I don't know."

Coolidge swung around and looked at Relyea. "You ever wonder who all those people are that are going to live out here?"

"No," said Relyea. "Never given it a thought."

"No one's ever going to live in the valley," Coolidge declared.

"All right, guys," Max Hoover said to the uniformed cops. "We'll take it from here. No pictures, okay?"

The corpse was female, and she lay facedown in the soft ground. The four cops stood looking at the body with great curiosity. There was no sign of injury—no blood, no trace of a wound—but she was embedded in the ground as if she had been pressed there by a giant hand.

"Now, that's one I've never seen before," said Eddie Hall, plainly amazed. "How about you, Max?"

"New to me, too," said Max, gazing down.

"Maybe they'll tell us something," said Relyea, cocking a thumb at a car bumping up the road.

"Bobby and Milt," said Coolidge. "My two favorite coroners."

The car pulled up to the site, and two coroners from the LA County morgue emerged. In Max's experience, coroners were more jaded and had sicker senses of humor than even cops.

"Hi, guys," said Bobby, the younger of the two coroners. "Beautiful day for a ride in the countryside, huh?"

"Gorgeous," said Coolidge.

The two coroners looked at the body critically with the air of connoisseurs, like art experts examining an old master painting for signs of forgery. They had seen just about everything in the death game—next to LA coroners, LA cops were just well-informed amateurs—but they had never seen this, either.

"How'd she get in the ground like that?" Bobby wondered aloud. He and his partner got down on their knees next to the body and dug with their hands around the body.

"So what happened?" asked Hoover.

"She died," said Bobby.

"Well, then," said Ellery Coolidge. "That's it. Case closed."

"The ground is awfully soft," said Bobby, still digging with his hands around the body.

Eddie Hall turned to the foreman. "You run the job?"

The foreman nodded. "This part of it, I do."

"Do you have some kind of machine here that could push a girl into the ground like that?" Hall asked. "You know, some kind of roller, like a steamroller."

"There's no roller on this job, not yet." The foreman scratched his head. "You could do it with a rover, I guess. But that would've torn her up really bad. She'd be a real mess if she got worked over by a rover."

"Beides," said Relyea. "How fast do those things move? No one just stands around and waits to get run over by a steamroller. That only happens in cartoons."

"Maybe she wasn't conscious. She could have been drugged and then flattened," said Hall.

"Why bother?" said Max.

"You know as well as I do, Max, people do some strange things," Eddie Hall replied.

"This is how you found her?" Max asked the foreman.

The foreman looked at him for a moment,

taking in Hoover's natty clothes. Then he nodded.

"Yes, sir. Right here. We didn't move her or nothing." The foreman glanced down at the body. "We found her just like this."

"Okay," said Hoover. "Just step over there. The officers will want to take a full statement from you."

Bobby was still feeling around the body, first under the elbows, then under the arms, then finally under the ribs.

"Jesus . . ." said Bobby, looking up from the body. "Milt? There's nothing to hold onto. It's like every bone in her body is broken."

"Roll her over," Hoover ordered. "Let's see what she looks like."

"Okay," said Bobby. "But you understand you're not seeing her at her best."

"Very funny."

The two coroners stepped over the body carefully and lifted the arms—but they bent in half a dozen places that arms aren't supposed to bend. The older coroner, Milt, dropped the arm, and it flopped like a dead fish. Bobby thrust his hands under the body and rolled it over.

The face had been crushed into an awful smile. But there was enough there to recognize the once beautiful features of Allison Pond.

Hoover glanced at her and then looked away,

trying to control the emotions that were surging through him. He stared out over miles of what will one day become a suburb.

"Max, you okay?" Coolidge asked.

Hoover swallowed hard and nodded. "Yeah," he said trying to put some steel into his voice. "Come on, let's go."

It took a few hours for the Los Angeles County coroner's meat wagon to get up to the murder site and retrieve the body, so it was late in the day before Hoover and Relyea got the call to go to the morgue for the autopsy on Allison Pond.

The postmortem room at the morgue was large and dark, and lined with gurneys each bearing a body, the heads to the walls, the feet—with toe tags—to the center of the room. On the wall above each body, numbers were chalked, each corresponding to the number on the toe tag. Some of the bodies were wrapped tight in white sheets like mummies, some were draped with white cotton, others were still wrapped in red field sheeting.

Hoover, Relyea, Milt, and Bobby stood over Allison Pond's ruined, naked body. Her skin was mottled and bruised, her once exquisite face broken and collapsed because the bones supporting it had been shattered and splintered.

Her dark hair had been combed straight back from her forehead.

Hoover touched one of her fingertips—they were black with fingerprint ink—and raised it, then let it fall. Even the bones in her fingers were broken.

"How did she die?" Hoover asked.

Milt shook his head slowly. "This is a real poser, Max. It's like she jumped off a cliff."

Hoover shook his head. "No, that can't be it. There's no cliff out there. Somebody moved her?"

"Nobody moved her," said Milt. "She died where you found her. That's one thing I can confirm."

"Who was that guy, Max," said Relyea. "You know the one . . . He used to beat people until their bones broke. He called 'em wheat cakes . . . Who was that?"

"Yeah," said Max. "I know the guy you mean. Walter. Walter Torre. He's still in the can isn't he?"

"Even if he wasn't," said Milt. "He isn't the guy. There's no blunt-force trauma here."

"Then, we're back to a roller," said Max. "A big piece of road equipment."

The older coroner just shrugged. "I don't know what to tell you on this one, Max. Sorry . . ."

Bobby was examining Allison Pond's wrists. "Hey, Milt, look here. A suicide attempt." There were ragged scars on both her wrists. Bobby peered at them through a magnifying glass. "Pretty sloppy work," he said.

Milt took a quick look at the scars. "Not recent," he said, "but they're not ancient, either. This young lady was pretty unhappy at some point in the last year or so."

Hoover stared at the old injury. Those scars had not been on her slim wrists when he had known her.

"Hey, Milt," said Relyea. "Did you get a look at this?" He was at the far end of the gurney, squatting down, examining Allison Pond's bare feet.

"What?" asked Milt.

"I think it's glass or something," said Relyea peering at her heel. "It's stuck in her foot."

"Let's see," said Milt. He moved to the feet, looking at the heel through a magnifying glass. He dug into the skin with a pair of sharp tweezers and pulled a sliver of something from her flesh. Milt held his tweezers to the light.

"What is it?" Relyea asked.

"You were right," said Milt. "It looks like glass."

* * *

Jack Ryan and the other hoods who had been treated to a trip down Mulholland Falls would not have recognized Maxwell Hoover at home. Neither would a lot of the cops who knew him.

After dinner every night, without fail, tough Max Hoover helped his wife do the dishes. Or rather, she helped him—he washed, she dried. It was a little spot in their evening when they exchanged the small details of their respective days, the kind of minutiae that would only be of interest to one's spouse.

But tonight they hadn't spoken much, Hoover working silently, methodically, but preoccupied with thoughts of Allison Pond. He washed the last of the dishes, rinsed it, and set it down on the rack next to the sink. As Katherine dried it, Hoover picked up the clean plates and began washing them all over again.

"Max?"

He looked at her but did not seem to see until he had traveled the long road back from his thoughts. "Yes?"

"How many times do you plan on washing the plates?" Katherine asked, a little amused at her husband's absentmindedness.

For a moment Hoover did not understand what his wife was talking about. Then he realized what he had done and smiled.

"I guess twice," he said. "You know, I thought there were a lot of them tonight. I guess I need a hobby."

But his absorption continued throughout the evening, right up until it was time to go to bed. Hoover lay in bed as Katherine went through her usual bedtime ritual, cleaning her teeth, brushing her hair. Wearing only her nightgown, she seated herself at her vanity and picked up a bottle of hand lotion. As she opened it, she watched her husband in the mirror. He was still and silent and, she got the feeling, only physically in the room. His mind was elsewhere, somewhere far away.

"Can you tell me about it?" she asked quietly.

Hoover shook his head. "No, Kay. It's work . . ."

"I gathered," she said.

He gazed for a long time at his wife's face in the mirror. "Come here, honey," he said finally.

Katherine smiled and lay down on the bed and kissed him gently. Hoover snapped off the light, and Katherine raised her nightgown, pulling it off over her head. He took her soft nude body in his hard hands and pulled her under the covers next to him.

6

"What do you mean they can't indict?" Eddie Hall shuffled the cards expertly as he spoke and dealt quickly. Coolidge stuffed a hot dog into his mouth and picked up his cards.

"They can't indict," Hall continued. "What kind of bullshit is that? The guy killed his parents. We've got his fingerprints on the weapon. I call that reason enough to indict. Hell, it's enough to convict, too."

"Don't waste your breath, Eddie," said Relyea wearily as he sorted his cards by suit. "They won't do it . . . case closed."

Coolidge swallowed his hot dog. "What's wrong with this country?" he wondered aloud. "A guy with an ax chops up his parents, and he doesn't get the gas chamber. How can you plea-bargain something like that?''

"Search me," said Relyea.

"There's got to be a payoff somewhere there," Coolidge concluded in disgust. Then, as if to console himself at all the injustice in the world, he picked up the lunch pail at his feet, extracted another hot dog, and started eating again.

"You know," said Eddie Hall, "I knew that district attorney back when he was nothing more than a bagman for that Jack Draga. He was a flunky way back then, and he's still a flunky now." He slapped a card on the table. "Deuce," he said.

"Hell," said Coolidge, "he's worse than that. Brenda Allen said he had a thing for dressing up in women's clothing when he used to pay a visit to her whorehouse. When he was at Brenda's, Mr. District Attorney liked to be called Miss Sophie. Can you believe that?''

"From him, anything," said Eddie Hall, who, in his years with the Los Angeles Police Department, had witnessed virtually every form of sexual depravity humans were capable of performing on themselves, to others, to animals, to vegetation, and to a variety of inanimate objects.

Relyea, however, a comparative rookie and a man who still maintained a shred or two of innocence, was shocked. "No kidding? Women's clothes, really? How did he become district attorney then, for Christ's sake?"

"The district attorney is an elective office, Arthur. Get yourself enough votes and any scumbag can be elected. Plain as day."

"Yeah, but even in a dress?" Relyea asked.

"You can't be DA in this town unless you're a perfect size six," said Coolidge swallowing the last of his hot dog. "They haven't taught you that in that law school yet?"

"Well, it doesn't make a damn bit of difference," said Arthur Relyea. "If they won't indict, there's no trial, no conviction."

"Who are they working for down there, anyway?" Coolidge demanded. "The district attorney or the Commie Civil Liberties Union?"

"Hey, it's the boss," said Eddie Hall as Hoover entered the squad room. "Nice of you to drop in."

"Funny," said Hoover, going through his mail. There wasn't much of it, and only one piece of interest. It was a manila envelope addressed to him and marked personal. He did not recognize the handwriting.

He tore the envelope open and upended the contents on the table: a roll of eight-millimeter film and a single piece of paper. There was nothing written on the paper except a single phone number. He didn't recognize that, either.

Grabbing the film, Hoover crossed into the hall. A small, tough-mouthed woman sat at a secretary's desk, smacking around an ancient Underwood typewriter. There was a cigarette drooping from the corner of her mouth.

"Miss Newburg, get me a projector." He held up the film. "I'm taking my boys to the movies."

Newburg stopped typing and pulled on the cigarette, squinting at Hoover through the smoke. "Miss Newburg? What kind of bullshit is that, Max? When did you stop calling me Esther?"

"I wanted to get on your good side."

"I don't have one," Esther Newburg muttered. "You haven't figured that out by now? You are one dumb cop, Hoover." In another time Esther would have made a pretty good cop herself.

"Come on, Esther, get me that projector, will you? I want to watch a film. Sometime today."

"We don't have a projector," Esther said, turning back to her typewriter and her cigarette.

"We've got to have one," said Max. "What about the one they use for training films. You know, like how not to get the clap and stuff like that."

"I already know how not to get the clap," said Esther.

"Esther, come on, you know what I mean," Hoover pleaded. "Just tell me where it is, and I'll go get it."

"Big of you, Max," said Esther. "But I don't know where the department's projector is because the department's projector has been stolen. You happy now, Hoover?"

"Stolen?" said Hoover. "From the police department." He leaned back into the detective's room. "Hey, Coolidge! Did you take the department movie projector home with you?"

"No," Coolidge shouted. "Why? Where is it?"

"Don't know," said Hoover. "Esther says that it's been stolen."

"Stolen . . . But we're all cops," Coolidge replied. "We should be able to solve that one."

"No cops leave the room," said Eddie Hall.

"Somebody took the projector out of the storage room," said Esther as she ground out her cigarette in an overflowing ashtray. "Whoever it was never signed it out and never brought it back." She put another cigarette in her mouth, sat back, lit it, and exhaled an extravagant amount of smoke. "Now, that's what I call stolen. What do you call it, Hoover?"

"That's stolen, Esther. I should know," he

said. "I'm a policeman . . ." He thought for a moment. "I'm also the thief. I just remembered, I took it home a couple of weeks ago."

"Good. Arrest yourself," said Esther.

"So now that's settled," said Hoover. "You're going to have to find one someplace else."

"Me? A minute ago you were going to get it."

"Changed my mind . . . Look, I think the chief's got one of them in the conference room."

"Get it yourself," said Esther. "I'm busy."

Hoover didn't hesitate. "Coolidge! Go get it and bring it here. We'll watch it in the file room."

7

They assembled in the cramped dark file room a few minutes later, waiting more or less patiently while Coolidge attempted to eat a hot dog and thread film onto a movie projector at the same time.

Esther strolled in. "If you guys are gonna watch dirty movies in here, you could at least have the good manners to invite me."

"How do you know they're dirty, Esther?" asked Relyea. "Maybe it's an opera."

"Oh, yeah, people mail a lot of operas to police detectives, Arthur." She shook her head as she lighted her cigarette. "I'm disappointed in you, Arthur, I would have thought you would be smarter than that."

"Don't be hard on him, Esther," said Eddie Hall. "He's still learning."

Hoover swiveled around in his chair. "How come, Ellery, you got a hot dog while you're threading a projector? Why do you have to eat while you're working? What is it with you, anyway?"

"Leave me alone," said Coolidge defensively.

"Why do you have to eat all the time?" Hoover asked. "Don't you ever get tired from all that chewing."

"I eat so I don't think about food," said Coolidge, still struggling with the projector. "It's a psychological thing."

Hoover got out of his chair and looked at the projector. "I think we have to bend the film in there. See? See where they put the marks? Stick your finger in there and bend it."

Coolidge tried to do as he was told, but his index finger, which was huge, just wouldn't fit. "Damn, I can't reach it."

"So you eat so you won't think about food," said Hoover skeptically. "I don't mean to go butting into your business, Ellery, but this psychiatrist, this guy they got you going to is in worse shape than you are. 'Course, that's just my opinion . . ."

"She, Max," said Coolidge. "The psychiatrist is a she. A girl.'' He continued to struggle with the projector.

"A female?" asked Hoover. "You're going to a headshrinker, pouring out your heart, and she's a she?"

"Yeah, so?"

"What are you? Nuts?"

"That's the problem in the first place, isn't it Ellery?" Eddie Hall called out, butting in as usual.

Coolidge threw up his hands in exasperation. "I can't get my finger in there," he said. "It just won't fit."

"Try your dick," suggested Esther Newburg helpfully.

"Hey, Newburg," said Hoover. "Don't you have something better to do? Like work?"

Esther shook her head. "Nope," she said. "There's something better to do than this?"

"Go file something," Hoover ordered.

"This *is* the file room, Max."

Hoover sighed and took a pencil out of his pocket and handed it to Coolidge. "I didn't know you were going to a psychiatrist because of food, Ellery. I thought it was for the other thing."

Coolidge stuck the pencil into the mechanism of the movie projector, threading it at long last. "They're related, Max," said Coolidge. "The anger and the eating. They come from the same place. I get mad, the food calms me down. I wouldn't say that's such a bad thing. Would you?"

Before Ellery Coolidge had found professional help, he had been subject to monumental and overwhelming rages. One moment he would be his usual, affable self. The next he would be in the clutches of a blistering fury. The violence he could do when possessed like that was truly frightening.

Coolidge checked the movie projector one more time. "There, I think did it."

"You got it?"

"Yeah."

"Let's go." Hoover snapped off the lights, and Coolidge started up the movie projector.

First there was nothing on the screen except a bright white square of light, then that was replaced with lurid color footage moving fast—so fast that it was difficult, at first, to make out what it was. Then it came clear. It was a landscape, the road flashing by and photographed at close range.

"Someone's just filming out of a car," said Relyea.

"I wonder if they even knew the camera was on," said Eddie Hall.

The shots of the road and the desert vanished

and were replaced with jerky, random shots of the Double Diamond casino. There was a shot of the white canvas canopy over the outdoor bar, a shot of the waitress bringing Jimmy Field's drink to the table, the pianist at his instrument. Then the camera calmed down and focused on Allison Pond as she made her way through the bar to the tables.

"Max?" said Coolidge. He did not turn, but kept his eyes squarely on the screen. Hoover, standing at the back of the room, did not respond. He, too, could not break his gaze.

Jimmy Fields handed the camera to Allison and suddenly his face appeared on the screen. He smiled and crossed his eyes. He disappeared, and there was a shot of the faroff atomic explosion and the mushroom cloud rising into the clear blue sky. The camera shook as the shock wave blew by them.

"Max?" said Coolidge. "She looks like the dead girl we found in the valley, doesn't she?"

The shots were becoming jerkier and shorter. There were views of the desert from a moving car again, then amateurish pans of a man in uniform. The figure was slightly out of focus, but it was apparent that he was older. And he was laughing at something, pointing at the lens as if accusing the person behind the camera of something naughty-naughty.

There was another man in uniform, but he was not laughing. He scowled at the camera and put his hand up to the lens to prevent his being photographed.

Next came a typical holiday shot, as the camera panned over purple mountains rising from the desert plain. That vanished in an instant, though, and was replaced by a shot of a low white building of a vaguely military appearance.

Then came the first jolt of the film. The camera entered a large room, and the lens swept it shakily. It was a white room filled with beds, a hospital room with a patient in every bed. The faces were dark and disfigured, some mouths open and twisted.

"What is this?" Esther asked, blowing a stream of blue smoke into the beam of light from the movie projector. "Somebody's summer vacation."

"If it is, it doesn't look like they had a very good time," said Hall.

"No smut yet, Esther," said Arthur Relyea.

A man appeared on the screen. He was dressed in nothing but boxer shorts, a sleeveless T-shirt, socks, and a cowboy hat. He was carrying a drink and speaking to someone off camera—as he was speaking to the four cops and Esther—but there was no sound, only the rackety hum and click of the movie projector.

"Here it comes," said Esther cackling. "You spoke a little too soon there, young Arthur."

General Timms looked directly at the camera for a moment, but he seemed not to be aware that it was there. He turned away and did a little dance step across the room, like a happy puppy.

Allison Pond appeared—she was naked—and walked to him. Timms smiled warmly at her. Even on the amateurish film, it was plain that there was love in his eyes. Allison took the glass from his hands, fished an ice cube out of it, and thrust her hands down the front of the general's shorts, touching the ice cube to his private parts.

"That'll wake you up," said Relyea.

The general was trying to pull away, but Allison would not let him escape from the pleasure she was giving him. His face was a mask, a mixture of pain and ecstasy, somewhere between torment and rapture.

"Do people really do this kind of stuff?" Esther Newburg asked no one in particular.

Allison still had her hand in General Timms's shorts, massaging him. She pulled his face close to hers, until there was only an inch or two between them. He tried to kiss her, but she would not let him, her head bobbing and weaving like a boxer's. Her hand was moving faster now, and his eyes closed, his chest heaving as he worked toward his climax. The cops and Esther could see that his body was as tense and as taut as a long piece of sprung steel.

Then Allison stopped and General Timms froze, so close to orgasm his frustration seemed to scream off the screen. Allison said something, and General Timms answered no, shaking his head as he did so. Then he dropped to his knees in front of her, and she pulled his face hard into the V between her legs.

"Max," Coolidge called out. "Does that guy look familiar? I know I've seen that guy somewhere, Max."

Hoover's answer was abrupt. He yanked the plug from the wall, and the screen went blank. Without a word he stalked from the room.

Coolidge looked around the room, puzzled at Hoover's sudden display of temper. "Esther, was it me? Was it something I said?"

Esther shrugged. "Search me . . ."

Hoover was slumped at his desk, still lost in thought. Coolidge approached warily, as if he did not want to spook a wild animal.

"Max?"

Hoover looked up, his eyes cold. "Ellery, I would like you to do me a favor. Okay?"

Coolidge nodded. "Okay . . ."

"I want you to get yourself something to eat

and go back to your desk. That's all I want. I don't want to hear a word. Understand?''

"That's not what I meant . . ."

"Well, that's the favor I want, Ellery."

"Max, if anything's wrong, you know . . . it can help to talk it over, to get it out in the open . . . You know, if it's anything like that . . ."

"It's nothing like that," Hoover replied. He knew that Coolidge was only trying to help out a friend in need, and he was touched by the gesture, but right then the only thing he wanted from Ellery was his absence.

"Ellery," he murmured, "please do me the favor . . ."

"But I know how hard it can be, Max." Coolidge looked genuinely upset. "Bottling things up is going to ruin you in the end."

"Ellery, please."

Coolidge nodded and reluctantly walked away. Hoover sat staring into space. His gaze fell on the ashtray, in it was the balled-up message from Allison Pond. He picked through the ashes and the cigarette butts that had accumulated in the ashtray since the day before, looking for the crumpled note. Carefully, he smoothed it out on the desktop. *Allison Pond—Please Call.*

He wished now he could.

He was still staring at the note when Esther Newburg leaned into the room. "Max," she said, "sorry to bother, but that thing with the ice that the girl did. You know, the ice on the dick?"

Hoover nodded. "Yeah?"

"Well, tell me straight," Newburg insisted. "Do men really like to have that kind of thing done to them."

"I don't know, Esther," Hoover replied.

"Do you know *anyone* who does that? I mean, do people really do that in real life?"

"I don't know, Esther." But both of his answers were lies. He wanted to say I know what it's like because she did it to me . . .

8

It was called the Seacoast Colony, a ramshackle collection of beach houses squeezed onto a strip of coastline up the coast highway, too far from downtown to attract any residents who worked steady. Seacoast was a hangout for beatniks, freaks and fruits, reefer smokers, and other runaways from polite society. Some movie people were beginning to move in, and the houses were getting more lavish and the land more valuable, but the Hollywood types were a lot like the original inhabitants—they liked drugs or to sleep with fellow members of their own sex.

Max Hoover pulled the Buick off Highway One and drove down toward the beach, stopping in front of a dilapidated bungalow perched on the sands, just yards from the ocean. Like all of the houses out there, this cottage turned its back on the land, as if the free spirits of the Seacoast Colony looked out to sea, giving the cold shoulder to the entire country that stretched all the way back to the stuffy Atlantic coast and what was still called the mysterious East.

Hoover got out of the car and looked around, walking toward the tumbledown single-story dwelling. He tried to peer in the small, shuttered rear windows, but all that he could see through the slit was darkness.

There was a rustling in the sea grass. "Hoover?"

Max Hoover turned and saw Jimmy Fields emerging from the scrub at the edge of the sand. He was carrying a small, cheap handgun down by his side. It was one of the shoddy small-caliber guns that were beginning to be seen down in East LA, the gangs giving up their bicycle chains and zip guns in favor of more powerful weaponry.

Max Hoover could imagine Jimmy Fields driving down to the barrio to buy the gun from some tough beaner on the street, sweating bullets as he traded his ten bucks for what he thought was protection. Fields didn't know, of course, that with a lot of those cheap firearms the safest place was usually in front of them.

"You alone, Hoover?" Fields asked, brushing the sand from the knees of his khaki pants.

"See anyone else?" Hoover asked.

Fields looked to the car, then up and down the beach. It was obvious that he was only slightly reassured.

"You remember me?" Fields asked.

"Should I?"

"I remember you, Hoover," said Fields, shaking his head. "I remember you real well."

"Yeah? How so?" Hoover was busy searching his memory. Fields's pretty-boy features certainly were familiar to him. When he looked at him, the image of Allison Pond came to him, but somehow he couldn't quite put them together.

"I was there that night," Fields replied. "I was at Kenny Kamins's place the evening Kenny unfortunately slipped into a coma in the middle of his own party. You must remember that night."

Hoover nodded. He certainly remembered a clownish hood called Kenny Kamins. He remembered Kenny's taste for young girls . . .

"So? What do you want from me?"

Fields half laughed and shook his head ruefully. "I need protection," Jimmy said. "And I need it now."

"Protection? From what?"

"Did you look at the film I sent you?" Fields

asked, as if that would explain everything. "I know you know the girl. Do you know who the guy is, Hoover? Ring any bells?"

Hoover shook his head. "I don't even know who you are."

"I'm Jimmy Fields, Hoover. And the guy on the film killed her."

Max Hoover didn't react. "Killed who."

Fields got angry. "Look, spare me the crap, would you Hoover? I don't have time for it. Our mutual friend. That's who. You know who I'm talking about, don't you? She's dead, and I know who killed her. And unless I get some help from you, I am going to end up going out the same way."

"How do you know she's dead?" Hoover asked. Allison's unpleasant little death was not the kind of thing that made the papers.

"She would have called me otherwise," Fields answered. "She always did. We used to talk three, four times a day. I was her best friend." Fields smiled. "And you know what that means? It means I was one of the few people that didn't fuck her or fuck her over."

"Yeah?" Hoover retorted. "What did you do with her, Jimmy? Share tips on makeup?"

Fields didn't get angry, in fact, he was rather pleased. The homosexual world in Los Angeles was still a shadowy one, even to a policeman, and overtly queer men like Fields were a rarity. It always amused him when rough, tough straight men like Hoover got edgy if they thought a little slip of a man like Fields was coming onto them. He got the feeling that Hoover would rather face a gunman in a dark alley than a kiss on the lips from a man.

"Do I make you nervous, Lieutenant?" Fields leaned in, lowering his voice as he spoke. "Or is there a little piece of you that worries you . . . That little voice that tells you that you might be the tiniest bit bent?"

"To tell you the truth, Mr. Fields, I don't care if you get down on your belly and fuck snakes."

"I know what you're thinking. What's it like? What would it be like to stick my dick in his mouth. Or his dick in my ass . . ." Fields was just inches from Hoover's face now, and he was tiny next to the huge cop. It was all Max could do to stop himself from pulling back. He could feel Fields's patchouli-scented breath like a sickly sweet breeze on his face. " 'Cause you see, Hoover, I've fucked a lot of straight men. You'd be surprised. A lot of straight men . . . Which means I've fucked a lot of snakes. Lots and lots of snakes."

For a moment Hoover was afraid he was going to lose his temper and hit Fields, but he could see that the smaller man was not afraid of him.

That impressed him. Most people were afraid of Maxwell Hoover.

"Okay, you want to cut the crap?" said Hoover. "Let's cut the crap. When was the last time you saw her."

It was as if neither of the two men could bring themselves to actually say her name out loud.

"Friday," said Fields. "Up in Las Vegas." Jimmy thought for a moment and then corrected himself. "No, it was Saturday. She dropped off my movie camera at the motel Saturday morning."

"How did she seem? Was she worried about anything," Hoover asked. "Was she upset?"

Fields shook his head. "Not at all," he replied. "Far from it. She said she and the general were going for a ride and that she'd see me back in Los Angeles. She looked great. She seemed happy."

Hoover shook his head quickly, taken aback. "Wait a minute," said Hoover. "A general? What general?"

Now it was Fields's turn to look as if he had been taken by surprise. "You didn't know?" He shook his head in disbelief. "You cops . . . You spend all your time rousting homos in North Hollywood and beating up bums and Negroes . . . Man, go look him up. He's a general all right. General Thomas Timms."

"She was seeing a general?"

"Didn't you watch the movie? I was sure that would get your attention. She was doing a lot more than seeing him, Hoover," said Fields. "The general is a man of . . . appetites. And so was she. The two of them were banging like screen doors. Couldn't keep their hands off each other."

"Don't talk like that."

Fields laughed. "Oh, now you're Lieutenant Sensitive. We both know what she was, Hoover. The difference is, I didn't care. I loved her, and you used her. All the men in her life used her."

"Including the general?"

"Particularly the general," said Fields. "She had this crazy idea he was going to leave his wife and marry her. She could be hard as nails, but she was a schoolgirl when she was in love. She felt things deeply, and when she got hurt, she got really hurt."

"Did this Timms tell her he was going to split up with his wife?" Hoover asked. "Did he give her hope."

"Ha, hope . . . Disappointment she could stand. She always knew it was the hope that would do her in." Fields looked at the ground, saddened by the talk of Allison. "She was such a fool . . . She really thought that General Thomas Timms was going to leave his wife, give up his career and his big-time job, and marry a Los Angeles chippy less than half his age. I think she could even see herself pouring tea for the other officers' wives."

Fields looked up, there were tears in the corners of his eyes. "I miss her, Hoover. We'd cheer each other up. We'd help each other when we were scared. Now I'm scared, and I have to turn to . . . you."

"How many more films are there?" Hoover asked.

"More than one."

"Did she know?"

"Know? Know what?"

"That you were taking movies of her," Hoover's voice was serious and heavy with threat. "I asked you a question."

Finally, Fields shook his head. "No, she didn't know about that."

Hoover cocked his chin at the gun. "Get rid of that. You're only going to hurt yourself." He started toward the car.

Fields raised his voice. "She got in the way of a powerful man, Hoover. She was a threat. She was inconvenient—and when she got inconvenient, they had to get rid of her."

Hoover continued walking and did not turn around, but he felt the words on his back like arrows.

"I'll say this for you, Hoover. At least, all you did was break her heart. You didn't kill her. She was going to do that for you, she was going to save you the trouble of pulling the trigger . . ."

This time, Hoover did stop. He turned and looked back at Fields, his eyes questioning.

"You didn't know, Hoover?" Fields called out. "She tried to kill herself when you left. I know, I was the one who took her to the doctor to get her wrists stitched up. She was a mess."

Max Hoover started for the car again.

"I need protection, Hoover. You're supposed to be a cop . . . I thought you couldn't turn anybody down."

"Is that what she said?" Hoover shouted.

"That's what she said."

"She was wrong," he called over his shoulder.

Jimmy Fields brought up the gun and aimed it squarely at Hoover's back. But he couldn't pull the trigger. He fired the gun in the air and then dropped it to the ground.

9

An almost empty bottle of Calvert rye whiskey between his legs, Max Hoover drove home with the slow, elaborate, labored care of a very drunk man.

He had started hitting the bottle early in the afternoon, the minute he got back to downtown Los Angeles. It started with a couple of rounds of drinks at the usual hangout, a bar run by a retired cop called Gus, with Coolidge, Hall, and Relyea—strong brown drinks washed down to the noise of a lot of laughs as Hall and Hoover traded war stories about LA the way it used to be. Through all the chortles and merriment, Allison Pond sat squarely on Hoover's mind. No amount of liquor and laughter could budge her.

The other three cops had drifted away, but

Hoover stayed on, drinking alone and becoming more and more morose. He was slumped across the bar until Gus threw him out, telling him that a drunk at the bar was bad for business.

That began a long bar crawl through greater Los Angeles as Hoover hit legal bars until they closed, then crashed a couple of illegal drinking establishments he knew of down around Culver City. He got a couple of drinks at a whorehouse in East LA, but paid no attention to the girls, and even got some booze at a card-and-dice den near Grand Central Airport.

Then he picked up his bottle of rye for the long trip home . . . The trouble was, Allison had been along all night, following him every step of the way. She had been in the smoky bars and the vice dens, shadowing him all the way across the long Los Angeles night.

He brought the Buick to a halt in front of his house, staggered across the lawn, and then trampled through the flower beds, the bottle in one hand, trailing his suit coat behind him.

Thinking he was being very canny, he slid his key into the lock, and with great care like a second-story man, he turned over the tumblers trying to duplicate the dexterity of a safe-cracker. He failed miserably, of course. The simple act of turning the key sounded as loud as an assortment of tin cans falling on hard asphalt.

Katherine was curled into a corner of the living room sofa, a drink, scarcely touched on the end table next to her. A book lay in her lap, her finger marking the spot where she had closed it over her hand. The television set was on, but she paid it no heed at all.

When Hoover entered the room, she did not get up, she didn't yell. She just shook her head slowly. "Drunk . . . as a skunk."

Max nodded. "That's right."

"And you walked through the flowers."

"How do you know?"

"I'm married to a detective."

Max looked down at his shoes and saw that the petals of Katherine's begonias and dog roses were plastered to the soles of his shoes. It looked like he had marched through a bouquet of flowers.

Hoover nodded again. "And I walked in the flowers."

Very carefully, he leaned down and plucked a few of the battered blooms from the soles of his shoes and tried to shape them into some sort of nosegay. He sat down heavily on the floor next to Katherine, wedging himself into the small space between the sofa and the coffee table. Then he proffered the flowers.

"For you," he said.

"They were already mine."

"Sorry," he said sheepishly.

He looked at the book on her lap. "*A Farewell to Arms* by Ernest Hemingway." Taking the book from her hands, he placed it on the coffee table next to him.

"The way that guy writes, you'd think he never talked to a woman in his whole life," Max Hoover announced with that curious certainty that comes of the extremely intoxicated.

Then, as if going to sleep, having just delivered the definitive word on the entire oeuvre of Ernest Hemingway, Hoover put his head down on his wife's belly. She touched his hairline lightly.

"So when did you read Hemingway?" Katherine asked.

"He has no understanding of the things that make a woman happy," Hoover murmured. "He thinks they all want to be called 'my darling.'"

Katherine raised an eyebrow. "Is that so?"

"Absolutely!"

"And you know what makes a woman happy."

"Yes I do."

"Well, what is it?"

"Well, I'll tell you." He lifted her skirt and placed his ear down on the bare skin of her stomach. He closed his eyes. "And what they

84

really want . . . is a man who will listen to their stomachs.''

"Don't drool on me, Max," said Katherine.

He lay still for a long moment. Then without opening his eyes, he spoke again, sounding serious and sober now.

"We found a dead girl out in the valley . . .'' he said slowly. Katherine did not speak, but she ran her fingers through his hair.

"She was broken in a hundred pieces," he said. "She was so badly broken up, they couldn't even pick her up.''

She continued to stroke his hair. He sighed and settled against her, like a shipwreck settling on the ocean floor.

"Who was she?" Katherine asked.

Hoover's eyes opened. There was a long, long pause before he answered, as if he could see Allison Pond. "Just a girl . . ." he said.

He closed his eyes again, and a moment later the alcohol and the grief washed over him, finally allowing him to sleep.

Very gently, Katherine eased his head off her stomach, slid out from beneath him, and slowly lowered his head onto the couch. She covered him with an afghan, then picked up his wrinkled jacket and turned off the television set. A sudden silence fell over the room.

Katherine looked at her sleeping husband awkwardly stretched out, half on the floor, half on the couch. She was sad for him and hated the demons he battled.

10

Coolidge, Relyea, and Hall fell in step next to Max Hoover as he walked down the sweeping stone steps of city hall.

"Tie one on last night, Max?" Eddie Hall asked.

"You were there, Eddie." The four men walked off the steps, crossed the sidewalk, and walked out into traffic, ignoring the sudden squeal of brakes and the horns of irate drivers.

"You were still there when I left, Max." He shot Hoover a glance.

"Besides," said Coolidge. "You look like shit."

."Now, don't go sugarcoating the pill, Ellery," said Hoover. "Let me have it with both barrels, and the hell with my feelings."

"Well, you do look like shit," said Relyea.

"Where are we going?" Hall asked.

"We're not going anywhere," said Hoover, making for the Buick. "I've got something to take care of. I'll be back later."

The other three men exchanged conspiratorial looks. It seemed that Hall had been elected spokesman for the group.

"We've been thinking . . ."

"Uh-oh," said Max. "That is always a bad sign. I hate to hear that."

"This is serious, Max," said Coolidge soberly.

"We've got to ask you a question, Max," said Hall. "Is this about the dead girl. Is she the same girl in the movie."

Hoover winced and looked angrily at Hall, Coolidge, and Relyea. The three men stared back. They were not going to give in on this.

"Who told you that?" Hoover snapped. "Wouldn't have been my old friend Ellery here, would it?"

Coolidge looked down, feeling guilty about betraying a confidence. "I've been worried," said Coolidge in his own defense.

"Worried?" Hoover asked angrily. "What the hell were you worried about, Ellery?"

"We're partners here, Max," said Coolidge. He was just as angry as Hoover now, and he didn't care if it showed. "Was there something between you and that girl. If there was something, you better tell us about it, goddamn it!"

Hoover turned and sighed, looking at Coolidge intensely. For a moment it looked as if he would break down and spill his confession. But the moment passed, and he backed down.

"Guys, I want you to cut me a little slack on this one," he said. "Just let me do what I have to do. Okay?"

The three men did not budge. Hoover shrugged and opened his door, and the others climbed in, taking their usual places.

"I thought you guys had grand jury testimony today," said Hall. "I thought I'd get you off my back for once."

Relyea was not worried. "Don't worry about the grand jury, Max," he said. "They can't indict on this one."

Hoover dropped the car into reverse and backed out of the parking space. Hall, feeling better that he was going along for the ride, stretched out luxuriously in the big seat, enjoying the warmth of the morning sunshine.

"So where are we going?" Hall asked.

"It's a surprise," said Hoover.

The convertible cruised up Vermont. Coolidge pulled a Baby Ruth bar from his pocket and unwrapped it. Then he leaned forward so his voice could be heard in the front seat.

"You know, I've been thinking . . ."

"Here we go again," said Hoover sourly. "You know, I'm really starting to hate it when you guys say that."

"What have you been thinking, Ellery?" Hall asked over his shoulder.

"Well, why is it we always sit in the same places? You know, here in the car?" Ellery asked earnestly. "And why is it, Max, that you're always the one that drives the car."

Hoover thought for a moment and then shrugged. "I guess it's because I've got the keys."

"But *why* do you have the keys," Ellery Coolidge persisted. "That's what I'm asking about. There's a reason for everything . . ."

"I have the keys, Ellery, because it's my goddamned car," Hoover roared. "How much longer are you going to see this psychiatrist!"

"Yeah, Ellery," Hall asked. "How much longer are you going to be talking like a fruit loop?"

"There's nothing wrong with going to a psychiatrist," said Coolidge in self-defense. "Lot's of people go to a psychiatrist."

"Yeah," said Hall. "And lots of them are fruit loops."

"No one is critcizing you, Ellery," said Arthur Relyea.

"I am," said Hall.

"We just want to know how much longer, that's all."

"I don't know," said Coolidge. "The whole process . . . It's open-ended. Sometimes this stuff takes years to work itself out."

"Years!" said Hall. "Jesus, God . . ."

"So tell me, Max, why is it you always drive?"

"Max?"

"What?"

"Let Ellery drive, please . . ."

When the Buick pulled up at the modest two-story apartment complex in Los Feliz, Ellery was driving. Relyea was in the front seat, Hall and Hoover were in the backseat, looking out of place. Coolidge put the car into reverse and inexpertly parallel parked, backing the car into an old Plymouth parked at the curb. It was the gentlest of bumps—no damage done, except to Ellery Coolidge's fragile ego.

"Ooops," he said, turning around. "Sorry about that, Max."

"You know, Ellery," said Eddie Hall. "This just might be the reason that Max always has the keys."

The apartment complex was a low, hacienda-style building, a three-sided structure built around the swimming pool in the center courtyard. A number of young women were lazing around the pool oiled up and soaking in the sun. Every one of them was gorgeous. And each one of them was always "on." You never knew when the next person to stroll by might be *the* producer, agent, or director who would promote a young girl from aspirant to starlet—and perhaps even beyond.

As the four big cops walked in, every eye was fixed on them. It was the "you never know" kicking in. One, a stunning blond in a blinding-white bathing suit jumped to her feet and coquettishly adjusted the straps of her bathing suit. She was showing off her terrific legs. She certainly caught Coolidge's eye.

"Jeez," he said. "What long legs . . ."

The blond stalked to the edge of the pool like a cat and jumped into the water. She came up smiling, looked at the four cops for a moment, and then breathed deep and submerged again.

Coolidge gaped at her. "What the hell is she doing?"

Relyea put his hand on Coolidge's shoulder, a reassuring sort of gesture. "Don't worry," Ellery. "She's just practicing . . ."

Hoover and Hall looked at Relyea, too. They had no idea what he was talking about.

"Practicing what?" said Hall. "She's practicing going down on a producer while underwater."

"Use your imagination, Eddie," said Relyea. "She's working on her underwater smiling."

"What for?" asked Coolidge.

"Because she wants to be the next Esther Williams," said Relyea. "The best underwater smiler in the business."

The other women continued to stare and preen as the men walked around the pool.

"What are they looking at?" Coolidge whispered. "You think they know who we are?"

"They think we're movie producers," Eddie Hall said out of the side of his mouth. "It's the suits we wear."

The woman in the pool broke the surface at the end of the pool nearest the cops. She was gasping for breath, but she held the smile on her perfect face. Hall turned to Relyea.

"You are an eerie kid, Arthur, you know that."

"Arthur," said Hoover. "Go find the manager of this place and tell him we want to go through an apartment." He turned to Hall and Coolidge. "You two go see if the girls heard anything. Find out if any of them knew her. Find out if she ever had any visitors that we should know about."

"Now, that's just my luck. Typical. I'm always the one who pulls the dirty duty," said Eddie Hall as he ambled toward the nearest pretty girl. He shrugged. "But protect and serve, that's my motto."

Hoover started up the stairs to the second floor as Eddie sat down next to a girl who was stretched out on a chaise. She smiled at him and wondered if this could be the one . . . You never know . . .

"I'm a police officer investigating a homicide," said Eddie Hall. "Mind if I ask you some questions."

The girl did her best to hide her deep disappointment. "Not at all."

"You know who you remind me of?"

"Who?"

Eddie Hall shook his head slowly. "Absolutely nobody," he said. "I've never seen anybody like you in my life."

"Oh, you!" she said with a laugh.

Relyea was passing by, the manager of the apartment complex in tow. "Smooth, Eddie," he said. "Very smooth."

11

Hoover walked along the outdoor corridor, heading for the far corner of the building, feeling for his keys as he went. He certainly looked like he knew where he was going.

He looked at the door for a moment, sighed, and then inserted the key in the lock. The door swung open, and he could see in an instant that the entire place had been thoroughly tossed, searched from top to bottom.

Furniture had been overturned, the linings slashed open and the stuffing yanked out. Hoover picked his way through the wreckage. In the kitchen he found that all of the shelves had been emptied of plates, pots, and pans. The refrigerator was open, and food had been swept onto the floor, the gluey remains of broken eggs pooled and dried on the pale blue linoleum. All the drawers were open, all the silverware dumped in the sink. The toaster was in ten twisted pieces.

Hoover stood in the kitchen for a long moment, then walked into the tiny bathroom. Same story. The entire contents of the medicine cabinet had been emptied into the sink, and the searchers had even gone to work on the toilet, digging into the guts of the water cabinet, the heavy lid shattered into a dozen pieces in the bathtub.

Hoover stood still, looking things over, touching nothing. He sighed heavily and wanted to leave, but he forced himself to move, walking down the dark hall to the bedroom. It was a room he knew well.

There was still a sheet on the bed, but both it and the mattress had been cut open with a long vertical slash. All of Allison's stuffed animals had been cut open and tossed aside, as if it was a slaughterhouse for huggy toys.

The bedside table had been turned over, the single drawer dumped. Hoover picked up a pair of panties and put them on the dresser. Even as he did it, he wondered why he was doing it.

Suddenly, a great weariness overcame him, and worn out, he sank down onto the bed. There was a picture on the floor, and he stooped to retrieve it. It was Allison, a little girl in pigtails grinning a baby-tooth smile at the camera. He looked at it and could discern the beauty that lay in her future. None of the ugliness she would endure, none of the pain or heartbreak could be seen. He felt a sharp stabbing pain in his heart.

Hoover couldn't look at the picture for longer than a moment or two. His eyes flicked to the venetian blinds, tracing the fractured pattern of light around the room as it ran its crazy course along the floor and up the wall.

He remembered that light. He remembered the dark bars of shadow and bright light on her smooth skin. He remembered the lightness of her hair as it grazed his chest. He remembered her face, looking at him with a frank directness, her mouth moving, trembling with passion. Her eyes closed in impatient anticipation of the ec-stasy yet to come to her.

He could see her arching her back as the pleasure hit like a cold wave. She collapsed into his embrace, their limbs entwined.

Hoover remembered the old passion, and it hit him like a hard punch to the head. He dropped back onto the bed, lowering himself onto the mattress, sinking into a sexual past. Her scent was still there, faint, but perceptible. He inhaled it, pulling her into his lungs like smoke and then exhaled heavily, thinking of

Allison, missing her terribly and hating himself even more.

The wall facing the bed was covered by a long mirror. He had seen himself reflected in it many times, the glass throwing back images of the passion he and Allison had shared.

But the mirror was different now. Hoover stood up to examine it. There was a spot of light in it, a dot that seemed to come from the room next door.

"Hey, Max." Coolidge bustled into the room. "Would you look at this? This is the room where that film was taken." His voice was jarring in the silence, as if he was profaning a sacred place. He looked around, taking in the ruined bed and the mirror on the wall. Coolidge picked up the photograph and studied it closely.

"You think this is the girl we found in the valley, Max?" He angled the picture to the light to get a better look at it. "It's funny, isn't it . . . ?"

"What's funny, Ellery?"

"Looking at pictures of people who are gone now," said Coolidge. "I mean, the girl who died, she would be a stranger to this little girl. She's got no idea of the things she's going to do. She doesn't know what's going to happen. She doesn't know that girl we found up there any better than we do . . ."

Hoover nodded. "We should find out more. I need the key to the apartment next door."

"Okay, Max. Relyea got all the keys from the building manager," said Coolidge, leading the way back to the corridor.

Relyea was waiting. "The manager says this Jimmy Fields was her best friend." Relyea glanced at his notebook. "The guy says he hasn't seen either one of them in a week."

Jimmy Fields's apartment was identical to Allison Pond's in layout, and it had been just as thoroughly ransacked. Jimmy Fields must have had a thing for clothes, because there were a lot of them. All of his clothes had been dumped on the floor, and the closet systematically dismantled, right down to the floorboards.

"Whatever it was they wanted," said Relyea, surveying the damage, "they wanted it bad."

"And they knew what they were doing. They did both apartments, and nobody heard a thing," said Coolidge. "They were pros, all right. They even thought to look in the refrigerator."

Hoover stepped up to the wall that the apartment shared with Allison Pond's place. On the far wall was the one-way mirror, a cloudy panorama of her ravaged bedroom.

"It was movies," said Hoover. "Movies like the one we got." A wooden camera tripod lay smashed on the floor, a destroyed movie camera lying next to it. Hoover stooped, retrieved the camera, and put it to his eye. Rotating the lens, he looked through the camera at the mirror. In Allison's bedroom he could see Hall, just standing there. He could have been admiring his own image in the glass.

Hoover tossed the camera aside and walked quickly from the room. He stopped in the corridor and leaned over the banister, breathing in the sweet air and trying to contain the riot of emotions flooding through him.

"Max, you all right?" asked Hall.

"I couldn't stay in there a moment longer," said Hoover. "For a moment there, I couldn't breathe."

"You want a cigarette?" Hall asked, proffering a pack of Luckies.

"Yeah . . ." Hoover took one, lit it, and sucked the smoke down greedily, as if it was nourishing.

"So tell me," said Eddie Hall in a matter-of-fact voice. "How long were you seeing her?"

Hoover realized that there was no point hiding it anymore. "Six months," he said quietly. "Every chance I got for six months."

"Jesus Christ," Hall muttered. "That means he's got you on those damn films as well."

Hoover nodded. "That would appear to be true . . ."

Coolidge and Relyea emerged from Jimmy Fields's apartment.

"Hey, you think this guy Fields is a little light in his loafers? There's some awfully fruiting stuff on the walls in there. Naked guys and—" Coolidge stopped talking abruptly. They could tell by the looks on Hoover's and Hall's faces that the confession had been made.

"Jesus!" said Coolidge. "It was you and her, wasn't it Max?"

Hoover bit his lip and nodded. "That's right, Ellery."

"Oh, Jeez . . . How did this happen in the first place?" Coolidge asked.

Hoover took a deep breath. "Do you guys remember Kenny Kamins . . . ?" he asked.

12

No one who knew what happened that night a year and a half before could forget Kenny Kamins. He had a chic, upscale apartment, a penthouse in Westwood all paid for with mob money. Kenny Kamins controlled a couple of union locals on behalf of the boys back east, and he had a profitable sideline peddling dope to junkies all over the city, from movie stars in Beverly Hills to hopped-up skells downtown.

Kenny liked to spend his money on parties, and he had them frequently. They were always the same: lots of booze, lots of pretty girls, a sprinkling of movie people, and a lot of Kenny Kamins's more presentable gangster friends.

Hoover and his boys were not invited. But they crashed the party anyway, strolling into the party as if they were the guests of honor. Every mobster in the room knew who they were—they just couldn't believe *where* they were.

"Who the fuck invited you?" asked one of the mobsters.

"Shut up. Where's Kamins?"

"Never heard of him," said the thug.

Wham! Relyea hit him so hard he dropped like a sack of potatoes.

"I guess you ladies never heard of him, either," said Coolidge.

A dozen lovely heads shook. In truth, many of them did not know who their host was. They just went where their madam told them to go.

The four cops waded into the middle of the crowd. "So where's the food?" Coolidge asked.

Two gangsters with two beautiful girls stood next to the hors d'oeuvre table. One of the gangsters was wearing sunglasses—although it was well after midnight—because he had once seen Dean Martin do the same thing at Chasens.

As Coolidge started demolishing a cake of caviar, the guy with the sunglasses grabbed him by the shoulders.

"What are you guys doing here?" the mobster demanded.

"Where's your fuckin' warrant," said his colleague.

Coolidge piled an inch of caviar on a cracker

and popped it in his mouth. He had a thoughtful look on his face. "You know, you guys don't sound like you're from around here. You from New York by any chance?"

"So what if I am?"

"That's funny," said Coolidge swallowing. "I'm from New Jersey myself."

"Like I give a fuck."

"Sorry," said Coolidge. Then he punched the mobster hard and fast, right in the glasses, the frames and lenses splintering and lacerating his skin. Lightning fast, Coolidge whipped a martini glass off the table and jammed the glass—gin, olives and all—into the other guy's face, the glass shattering as it hit bone.

As the blood flowed and the two mobsters clawed at their cutup faces, the women in the room began to scream. Coolidge seemed genuinely surprised at the reaction, and he stepped back and shrugged, as if he had unwittingly committed some terrible social faux pas.

"Coolidge!" Hoover shouted. "Ease off, okay."

"Okay, okay," said Coolidge. "Everybody relax. Nobody got hurt. Hey, Max, he started it."

"Relyea, make him a drink," Hoover ordered. "Ellery, I want you to put your hand around something you can't hurt."

"What's your pleasure, Coolidge?" said Relyea. He went behind the wet bar, dislodging a small, handsome, well-dressed young man he would later come to know as Jimmy Fields.

Coolidge looked over at the bleeding gangsters. "In honor of these visitors to our fair city, make mine a Manhattan."

Hall laughed and walked up to one of the girls. "Honey," he said, "I think it's waaaay past your bedtime . . ."

Hoover walked down the hall of the apartment and stopped outside a closed door. Cautiously, he opened it and entered. It was Kenny Kamins's bedroom, a luxurious riot of black silk and zebra skin. The bed was huge, and there was a mirror on the ceiling. It was just the kind of strenuous, supercharged bad taste that Max Hoover would expect of a hood like Kamins.

There was no one in the room, but he could hear voices in the lavish dressing room next to the bedroom. With all due precaution, Hoover peered around the door and saw three people. One was Kenny Kamins wearing a smooth tuxedo. The other two were heart-stoppingly beautiful girls. One was in her twenties, dark-haired, green-eyed. The other, standing behind the woman as if being shielded from her, really was a girl. By Hoover's eye she could not have been more than thirteen.

"You can't do this to her," said the older woman adamantly. "She's nothing more than a kid."

"And so were you once, doll," said Kamins. "And look at what a beautiful woman you've become."

Hoover maneuvered a little closer. Kamins had his back to him. He could also see the works—the paraphernalia for cooking up heroin on the table next to the door. There was a long, evil syringe, too, the cylinder filled with the drug.

"You really are slime, Kenny" said the older woman, her voice filled with loathing. "You know that, Kenny."

The little girl behind her whimpered.

Kenny Kamins had run out of witticism. "Don't you talk to me like that you little tramp." He slapped the woman hard in the face, the smack leaving a livid red imprint of her creamy smooth skin. But instantly, she slapped him right back, a stinging blow to the face. He grabbed the syringe and threatened both girls with it.

The woman plainly had no idea how close she was to getting killed. Hoover stepped into the room. The woman saw him first, and Kamins following her gaze whipped around. When he saw Hoover, he dropped the syringe.

"Kenny, Kenny, Kenny . . ." Hoover shook his head slowly, as if he were a disappointed parent catching his son sneaking an illicit cigarette. "What are we going to do with you?"

"Lookit, Hoover," said Kamins. "This is a private party. Where's your goddamn warrant?"

"Everyone keeps asking for that damn warrant," said Hoover, his hands going through his pockets. His face brightened.

"I've got this." He pulled a black leather sap from his pocket. It was a small, flat black mean-looking piece of leather and lead. "Do you remember this, Kenny? I think you've met . . ."

Kenny's eyes widened, then suddenly he lunged for a small silver gun on a shelf. But he didn't make it. Hoover slammed the sap down on Kamins's hand. Well-manicured fingers cracked and snapped like pretzels.

"Jesus Christ!" Kamins screamed as he buried his injured hand in his stomach and folded himself over it. Hoover grabbed him and slammed him to the ground, pinning him there. Then he reached for the syringe and raised it like a dagger.

"Horse, junk, smack, scag, black tar, Mexican mud . . . What do you call this candy, Kenny?" said Hoover. "There are so many names . . . gum ball, peanut butter, Tootsie Roll, dog food . . . Can you think of any others, Kenny?''

"You are fucking crazy, Hoover,' Kamins said through clenched teeth. "Completely fucking crazy!''

Hoover looked up at the two girls. "Get her out of here.''

The older woman nodded and took the girl out of the room.

"So what do you say, Kenny . . . ?'' whispered Hoover. "What do you say we have a little party of our own. You seemed so anxious to offer some of this shit to your guests. Why don't you sample some yourself?''

Kamins was really sweating now. "I don't touch that stuff, Hoover,'' he said quickly. "You know that.''

Quietly, the woman stole back into the room and stood in the doorway watching Hoover and Kamins.

"You don't want to see this,'' said Hoover.

The woman nodded. "Yes, I do.''

Kamins's eyes swiveled in his head as he tried to see her. "Jesus Christ . . . Allison, call the cops.''

"I am the cops, Kenny . . .''

Hoover wrenched the man's head to the side, exposing the jugular vein. He struggled valiantly, but he could not break Hoover's hold on him. His eyes bulged from his head.

"Hoover! What do you want? You want money?"

Hoover's answer was simple. He jabbed the needle into Kamins's bulging veins and shot the whole column of brown liquid into him. The heroin flew through Kamins's bloodstream and hit his brain like a wrecking ball. Kamins's eyes rolled back in his head; then his body convulsed, and he began to shake uncontrollably. Hoover stood up slowly and looked at the woman.

"Are you always so inventive with the way you go about dispensing justice," she asked coolly.

"It's an integral part of the job," said Hoover.

"You were a little more effective than I was . . ." She looked down at Kenny Kamins. The tremors continued to wrack his body. "Cigarette?" She opened a slim silver cigarette case.

He took one and leaned forward for a light. Hoover exhaled and then offered the lit cigarette to her.

The woman shook her head. "Not now. It dulls the nerves," she said.

"You like to be nervous?"

"I don't like to be dull."

"So . . . who are you?"

"You won't find out by killing me."

"Killing you?" said Hoover. "Why should I kill you."

The woman glanced down at the body of Kenny Kamins. "You seem to have a knack for it."

"He's not dead . . . Tell me your name."

"It's Allison Pond . . ."

And that had been the beginning of it. She was beautiful and passionate, and Max did not have the strength to resist the voluptuousness of the sex they had together. She was calm and fearless and without inhibition. Max felt himself swept away by her beauty and her ardor.

For years to come, Hoover would wonder if he had killed Kenny Kamins just to impress her.

The memories made him sad, her death an unbearable sadness. The bright California sun, the laughs of the pretty girls around the pool, his wife, his friends . . . He felt as if he would never be happy again.

"Why did you fall for her, Max?" Coolidge asked.

"I was weak," he said.

13

They were all back in their proper places in the Buick. Max was driving, and Coolidge hadn't said a word about it, but he was anxious to talk to Hoover about other things.

"Can I ask you a question, Max?"

"What's it about."

"It's about your . . . It's about what happened . . ." said Coolidge suddenly feeling like a voyeur. "What did Katherine say? You're still together, so you must have worked it all out . . ."

Hoover was silent. His eyes flicked to the mirror, and he looked back at Coolidge reproachfully.

"You *did* tell her, didn't you?"

"Coolidge," said Hall. "Drop it . . ."

"No," said Hoover. "I never did . . ."

"What did she do when you told her it was over," Hall asked. "Was it a bad scene?"

Hoover shook his head. "No," he said. "She just said she understood. She said that it had been fun . . ."

"And then she just walked away?" asked Relyea.

"Well, yeah, sort of . . ." said Hoover. "She called a couple of times, but there wasn't any point. If I had seen her again, I would have left Katherine, and I couldn't take that chance."

"You never would have left," Coolidge insisted. "I can't believe you would leave a woman like that."

"You don't know, Ellery. You can't know until you find yourself in the same situation."

"There was a message to call her last week," said Hoover sadly. "I didn't, of course . . . I wish I had now." The thought of Allison in danger and that he could have helped her sickened him.

"Maybe it was something else," said Hall, trying—and failing—to sound reassuring.

"Max," said Relyea, "the scars on her wrists . . . the one's Milt and Bobby mentioned at the autopsy . . ."

"What scars?" asked Coolidge.

Relyea drew his index finger across his left wrist.

"I didn't know about that," said Hoover. "That was a little later, I guess."

"They say that's a cry for help," said Coolidge. "My psychiatrist told me that."

"Well," said Hoover. "She didn't cry to me. She cried to Jimmy Fields."

"That guy with the camera," said Hall. "You said he's a fruit, right?"

"You should have seen his apartment," Coolidge called from the backseat. "Fruit ain't the word for it."

"The guy isn't shaking you down is he?" asked Relyea. "Would he have the nerve to try that?"

Hoover shook his head. "No. He's too scared."

"We could go pay him a visit," said Relyea. "Just to make sure he doesn't decide to be a wisenheimer."

"I thought we weren't going to do that anymore," Coolidge protested. "We agreed no more Mulholland Falls."

"Shut up, Ellery," said Eddie Hall. In Hall's mind the Mulholland Falls routine was a very effective crime-fighting tool. The fact that it was, itself, a crime—that was another matter. But

Eddie Hall wasn't about to lose a minute of sleep over it, one way or the other.

"Forget it, Ellery," said Hoover. "It's not going to happen. Not to Fields, anyway. He's far from being the problem. He's scared, but I'll tell you one thing he's not scared of—me."

"I am," said Hall.

"Like hell you are," said Hoover, smiling for the first time that day.

Hall looked at Hoover in a flat, almost challenging sort of way. Relyea and Coolidge exchanged a quick glance. Hoover finished his cigarette and flicked it over the side.

"Any of you guys ever heard of a General Thomas Timms?" Hoover asked as he reached for another cigarette.

"You smoke too much," said Coolidge.

"You eat too much," Hoover shot right back.

"Timms?" said Relyea. "Yeah, I've heard of Thomas Timms. What's the matter, don't you guys read the papers?"

"I read the other day that there's a rumor that the Dodgers are going to leave Brooklyn and move out here," said Hall. "Now, that's news."

"It's also bullshit," said Coolidge emphatically. "You know as well as I do the Dodgers will leave Brooklyn the day lots of little green men hop out of spaceships and say take us to your fuckin' leader."

"What do you know about Timms, Arthur?" Hoover asked, ignoring the Brooklyn versus Los Angeles Dodgers controversy. "Tell me."

"Timms is one of the inventors of the A-bomb," said Relyea. "He was on the Manhattan Project from the beginning. First in New York. Then up in Los Alamos in New Mexico. He was appointed head of the Atomic Energy Commission just last year. Now he's Chairman General Thomas Timms."

"Really?" asked Hall.

"No. It was a joke."

"College boy," sneered Hall.

"Well," said Hoover. "What we have on our hands here is a dead girl. And that dead girl we have on seven minutes of film is Allison Pond. And the question is, what do we plan to do next."

Coolidge, Hall, and Relyea were quiet for a moment, turning this particular equation over in their minds. The silence was finally broken by a few cogent words from Eddie Hall.

"Then, I would say we've got problems, Max," he said.

Hoover hit the gas, and the Buick picked up speed, the huge V-8 engine pumping out a throaty, powerful roar.

"Where are we going, Max?" Relyea asked.

"Back to the office."

"Well, that's no fun," said Eddie Hall in disgust.

"I want to send a couple of uniforms to pick up the fruit."

"You know where he is?" asked Coolidge.

"Yeah. He's at the beach."

14

Hoover and Fields sat across from each other in a drab police interrogation room at the central police station in downtown Los Angeles. There was a full ashtray between them, and the air in the cramped room was heavy with the fug of cigarette smoke mixed with an undertone of sweat and fear.

Fields inhaled his cigarette and made a face. "I wish you'd send out for some Old Golds," he said.

"What do you think this is?" Hoover replied. "The Biltmore?"

Fields looked around the unpleasant little room. "I would never mistake this shit hole for the Biltmore, Hoover." He sighed heavily and pinched the filter off the butt and put it to his mouth again. It was apparent that the two men had been together for some time.

"How long are you going to keep me here?" Fields asked. "You can't hold me against my will."

"Yes I can," said Hoover. "Jimmy, I can do anything I want. Don't make the mistake of thinking I can't. I could pin anything on you I want. I could send you to the chair for the murder of Allison Pond." Hoover took a quick puff on his cigarette. "I could probably nail you for the Lincoln assassination if I wanted to."

"But . . . That's evidence planting. You can't do that! That's illegal. You'd never get away with it."

Hoover shook his head. "When are you going to get it, Jimmy? This is Los Angeles. The police can do anything they want. As long as all the nice folks in their nice houses aren't bothered by people like you."

"I have rights!" Jimmy protested.

"No you don't, Jimmy. No you don't." Hoover ground out his cigarette. "The minute you had sex with a man, Jimmy, you left yourself open to anything I want to do to you . . ." Hoover sat back and looked at Jimmy. "You know, you're right. I probably couldn't hang the Lincoln assassination on you, I probably couldn't even get you for the Lindbergh kidnapping. But I could get you for second-degree sodomy and throw it in front of Judge Gamel—pillar of the community and well-known fruit hater—and you'll go to the Q for three years." Hoover sniped another butt from the pack and lit it. "Now, are you going to cooperate, or not?"

"I *am* cooperating."

"Wrong question," said Hoover. "My mistake. I should have said, are you going to tell the truth? Are you going to be straight with me?"

Jimmy Fields had to giggle. "Straight with you? Well, that would be a first, Hoover."

Hoover even smiled. "Come on, Jimmy. You know what I mean."

"Okay."

"Let's go over it again . . . What did she say?"

Fields's deep sigh suggested that he was completely fed up with this process. "She said they were going for a ride. She and her general."

"And where were they going?"

"Out to where they test those things," said Fields. "Way out in the desert someplace."

"And she wasn't acting scared, edgy. Maybe she was acting nervous about something."

Fields smirked. "I guess you really didn't know her too well, did you, Hoover? Allison was never scared"—he stopped himself. "No, there was one thing that terrified her. She was terrified of being alone."

"I didn't know that."

"There's a lot you don't know . . . She wasn't scared of Timms, but she should have been. She thought he was protecting her."

"If she thought she was being protected, then what did she want with me?" Hoover asked.

Fields laughed sardonically. "I guess we'll never know that, will we?"

Hoover sat dead still. Fields stopped laughing as quickly as he started. "He killed her."

"What makes you think that?"

"You've seen the film," said Fields. "You tell me."

"I'm curious, Fields," said Hoover. "Why did you make those movies. Blackmail? Was that the idea?"

"Well, I thought about that," Fields replied. "I thought it might be nice to have a little something for a rainy—"

Hoover's hard hand whipped out and smacked him in the face. "I want you to tell me the truth, Jimmy."

Jimmy held his face and looked down. "What did you do that for?"

"Tell me why you made the movies, Jimmy."

"It made me feel part of it . . ." said Jimmy. "You know, I liked to watch the boys. Watch them get all worked up."

"You shot the film of me, didn't you?" Hoover asked. "What happened to that?" The thought of Jimmy Fields getting his kicks from watching him was unsettling.

"That's the question, isn't it? When Allison did not come back from the desert, I went back to the apartment. They had torn the place up, and they took all of the movies. Except the one I sent you. That was still at the lab."

"And that's the one they want," said Hoover. "But none of this proves Timms killed her."

Fields threw up his hands in disgust. "What do you need, Hoover? A road map? They know about the film—you said it yourself. Timms was the last person to see her alive. She's dead. They killed her up there!"

"She didn't die in the desert," said Hoover. "She died right here. Just outside of LA."

Fields did a double take. "She what?"

"You heard me."

Fields snapped the filter off another cigarette and lit it. Hoover noticed that the man's hand trembled as he held the match.

"*You* were the last to see her alive," said Hoover, leaning in close. "How do I know you didn't kill her?"

Fields jumped to his feet. He was red in the face. "Me! I didn't kill her! I was her best friend! I loved her. I took care of her, for

Christ's sake. I took care of her when people like you were abusing her, using her."

"Hey," said Hoover. "Simmer down there."

"Shut your face, Hoover!" Fields was shouting now. "She nearly died after you left her. She loved you, and you abused her. You guys are all alike. You think you protect the innocent, but you beat up on the weak or anybody that might stand in your way. You know, I was wrong about you. You *did* kill her. If anyone was responsible for Allison's death, it was you, you son of a bitch! You killed her!"

Fields's anger boiled over, and the intensity of his rage overcame him. He threw himself on Hoover, smacking his fists against his chest and stomach. Hoover was as angry as Fields, he picked up the small young man and slammed him against the cinder-block wall of the interrogation room, snapping his head against the ungiving brick, slamming his forearm—heavy as an iron bar—across Fields's throat. Hoover's face was a mask of fury, and he seemed to be hell-bent on squeezing the life out of Jimmy Fields.

The door slammed open, and Coolidge, Relyea, and Hall dove into the room. They were not there to come to the aid of Hoover, but to prevent him from doing really serious harm to Jimmy. They dragged Hoover off him, and

Jimmy fell to the dirty tile floor rubbing his neck and gasping for air. Hoover backed off, straightened his rumpled suit, and tried to get his anger under control.

"Come on, Max," said Coolidge, standing between Hoover and the hapless Jimmy Fields. "Get a grip on yourself."

"I'm okay," said Max. But his eyes still were inflamed with anger, and he stared at Fields as a predator eyes its prey.

Hall and Relyea helped Fields to his feet. "You are crazy, Hoover," Fields said hoarsely.

"Shut up." Hoover turned to Hall. "Eddie, you and Relyea take him out to the beach house. Take Earl with you. We're going to have to watch this guy twenty-four hours a day."

"Where are you going?"

"Ellery and I will come out later, okay?"

"Got ya. Come on Arthur."

Coolidge followed Hoover back into the squad room bull pen. "You ought to get it out, Max," he said. "You ought to talk to Katherine about what happened . . . It's understandable, it happens. Everybody's got weak moments once in a while. It helps to acknowledge them." And then, as if to declare his own weakness, he sat down at his desk and picked up the enormous corned beef sandwich he had been eating and took a big bite.

"Your psychiatrist tell you that?" Hoover asked slowly.

His mouth full of sandwich, Ellery could only nod his head.

"Let me tell you how it goes, Ellery," said Hoover. He could feel his anger reigniting. "It's like this: you meet somebody, maybe she's a little off center, but she tells you the truth, she stands up when she sees something wrong, and you like her for that. Understand so far?"

Coolidge cleared his mouth, swallowing quickly. "Uh-huh." He held the sandwich in his hand but did not resume eating it.

"One thing leads to another, and you end up in bed with this person." Hoover paused for a moment, looking straight into Coolidge's eyes. "Now, that's weak, I know, but nobody gets hurt. But you go home afterward and tell your wife, that's weak, too, but it's also cruel." Hoover paused again as if giving his words time to sink into Coolidge's consciousness.

"So here's something for you that doesn't cost you twenty bucks an hour, Ellery. You've got to carry your own water."

Without warning Hoover swung his arm, and with a backhanded slap he smacked the sandwich out of Coolidge's hand. It shot whole for a second, then disintegrated in midair, bits of meat and pieces of mustard-smeared bread flew across the room and fell to the linoleum.

Hoover immediately shook his head, regretting what he had done. "I'm sorry, Ellery," he said.

"I'm sorry, too, Max."

"Forget it . . . Let me buy you another sandwich."

15

When the dishes were done that night, Max Hoover took a bottle of beer from the refrigerator and descended to the basement. He unearthed the projector, smiling ruefully at the very clearly printed words on the label of the case: "PROPERTY OF THE LA POLICE DEPARTMENT. DO NOT REMOVE FROM SCREENING ROOM."

He threaded in the film and turned on the machine, the picture being projected on the dusty white wall of the basement. He studied the film closely, even the random shots of the desert, the weird scene in the hospital, then to the scene with General Timms.

Putting the beer bottle to his lips, Hoover drank a slug. He rocked the chair onto its two rear leg, his eyes never leaving the screen. In the flickering light Max Hoover's face looked drained and exhausted, but unable to turn away from the screen, powerless to drive the image of Allison Pond from his mind.

He did not hear Katherine enter the room behind him.

On the screen Allison was taking the ice from General Timm's drink and holding it to his penis. She watched the general's face as she held the ice against him, enjoying his tense pleasure for a moment or two. Then she raised her hands and put them on his shoulders, pushing him down, guiding him, until he is on his knees in front of her.

Katherine watched, transfixed, without a word, standing just behind her husband. Her eyes were wide.

Allison took hold of the general's head and pulled it into her, to between her legs, and held it there. She smiled and gazed down at him, her eyes very bright and full of affection.

"Who is that?" Katherine asked. Her eyes did not leave the screen.

Hoover was startled by the sudden intrusion into his trance. "It's all evidence," he said.

Katherine glanced at him quickly, then looked back to the screen. "The girl there . . . is she the one in the valley. The one who was all broken up?''

Hoover looked back to the screen. This was a part of the movie he had not seen. Allison's hold on the general's head had changed. Now she had her fists in his hair, and she was grinding against his face, urgently straining toward her orgasm.

"That's the girl," said Hoover quietly.

"She's so beautiful," Katherine replied.

On the screen Allison let out her silent cry of pleasure as her hips bucked and quivered . . .

The film ran out but the reel continued to spin, the film slapping as it whirled around. Without a word Katherine left the room. Hoover watched her go.

Katherine and Max did not speak much for the rest of the evening. They did not talk about the movie they had seen, they did not discuss the case or the death of Allison Pond.

At bedtime Hoover stood before the bathroom mirror, brushing his teeth. He was bare-chested. As he looked in the mirror, he could see his wife behind him. She wore her bra and panties and nothing else.

As he watched her, she approached, looking over his shoulder, their two faces framed in the mirror. Her fingers lightly massaged the tight muscles in his shoulders. Then she lowered her lips to his skin and kissed him hard, her fingers drifted down over his chest and stopped at his nipples. She squeezed them, teasing them to erection.

They were watching each other in the mirror as she played seductively with both nipples, then one hand moved downward, snaking around his waist to his crotch. Hoover shuddered as her hand closed around his shaft. His breathing deepened.

Katherine moved her other hand until they were both buried in his crotch. She pressed her breasts into his back, wrapping herself around her husband's waist. They gazed into the mirror, she was seducing him with the eyes and, like Allison on the film, watching him, enjoying the sight of him in ecstasy. Enjoying the power. She licked her lips seductively.

Suddenly, Hoover lost control, giving in to the flood of pleasure and passion. He turned and grabbed his wife, kissing her passionately, his tongue plunging into her mouth. She sucked it into her, their mouths open wide. He backed her against the door frame as Katherine wrapped her legs around him, climbing him.

Holding her in his arms, her feet locked behind his back, Hoover whirled around and into the bedroom. As they collapsed onto the bed, animal passion kicked in. They shed their few clothes in a split second, Hoover burying his head between her shapely breasts. She held his head tightly and moaned as his tongue flicked over her nipples, then she fell backward on the bed, carrying him with her.

Their need for each other was all consuming. She spread her legs wide, and he was in her, slicing through the slick soft folds and burying himself deep. Katherine's hips jerked forward hard, as if shocked, then she buckled her ankles behind his hips and her hands grabbed his chest, her fingers playing with the hard plates of flesh now oily with sweat.

The intensity of their twin orgasms surprised them both. Katherine gasped and dug her heels into the small of his back, twisting under him, grinding herself against him. Hoover fell forward onto her, combing his fingers through her fine hair.

Katherine smiled in the semidarkness and whispered in her husband's ear. "You know," she said, "you ought to bring your work home more often."

Relyea checked and rechecked the locks on the windows and doors of Jimmy Fields's beach house. For the most part the bolts were flimsy and corroded by long exposure to the salt air and would not keep out anyone who was really determined to get in.

Eddie Hall was stretched out on a rattan couch in the living room, trying not listen to the endless crash of the waves. He was also trying not to listen to Earl, who was with Jimmy Fields in the kitchen, the room adjacent. The aroma of pretty good cooking wafted out along with Earl's loud voice.

"Cooking is an art, you know," said Earl. "I don't mearue nothin'—I do everything by eye and color."

"And what color is that?" Fields asked.

"Bet it's brown," Hall yelled from the living room.

"Course it's brown, you jackass," Earl shouted back. "It's chili." Earl turned to Fields. "Pay no attention to him," he said as he diced a tomato with surprising dexterity, and slid it off the cutting board and into the bubbling vat of chili cooking on an old-fashioned gas range.

"These are Hollywood Reds, these tomatoes; they're the best. But the key is in the onions. Gotta have a lot of them . . ." He held up a handful of bright green jalapeño chillies and then started chopping them fine.

Fields looked puzzled. "Those aren't onions."

"Naww, that's just what we called 'em in the

service. That's where I learned to cook." The big cop dumped the fiery shreds into the pot. "Hm-hm, that's good. You gotta be a pepper belly to have good chili . . . That's the key. The Johnny Round Eye, it's gotta make you cry."

"Mind if I ask you a question?" said Fields.

"Shoot, kid."

Fields looked at him, taking in his scuffed shoes, his baggy pants shiny in the seat, his sack of a jacket and frayed tie. "So tell me. How come they dress so well, and you have to dress like that."

Earl laughed good-naturedly. "It all started with Max Hoover. He's always been a classy dresser. The others followed his lead." He thrust a handful of cutlery at Fields. "Here. Do something useful. Go set the table."

As Jimmy crossed the living room, Eddie Hall's eyes locked on him, following him as if he expected the young man to pull a gun or make a sudden break for it. Fields could feel the animosity radiating off the detective like heat.

"Would you take your shoes off my couch, please," said Fields as he passed.

"Go to hell," said Hall, but he did put his feet on the floor and sat up straight. "I don't know how anyone can live by the beach. Those waves always flopping and crashing around like that; it would drive me crazy."

Relyea nodded in agreement. "I'm with Eddie on that one. I like the sound of traffic when I'm sleeping."

Fields looked out at the dark ocean. "I find it very peaceful," he said. "So do most people. Maybe cops are different."

Hall grimaced. "Don't push your luck, Fields. The only reason we're here is because Max told us. If I had it my way, I'd toss you out of a speeding car, just to see if you'd bounce, okay?"

"You know," said Fields with a disgusted sneer. "You really are some kind of animal."

Hall's voice hardened, and he stood up slowly. "Don't make the mistake of messing with me, sonny. It wouldn't take too much to break you over my knee like a two-by-four."

Relyea stood and got between the two men. "Okay girls, simmer down. Let's not spoil this special evening . . . Hey, Earl!"

"What?" Earl called from the kitchen.

"How's the chili coming?"

"It's just about done," he said, emerging from the kitchen carrying a steaming pot. "As my Aunt Mabel used to say 'presentation is everything . . .' " He put the pot down on the table. The other three men looked in.

"Presentation is everything?" said Hall. "It looks like a bucket of mud."

"You trying to hurt my feelings?" Earl asked.

"Naww, nawww," said Hall. "Between you and Coolidge, I think you two should open an automat. You cook, and Collidge can be the customer."

"The way it looks is connected to the way it tastes," said Earl, gazing down at his creation.

"Then, this is really gonna be good," said Hall sarcastically.

Everyone else sat down, Relyea and Hall taking off their sacred suit coats, fearing that a single drop of Earl's toxic chili might land on them. Earl stood to dish up the chili.

He picked up a bowl and ladled a scalding dollop of chili into it. In that moment the night was shattered by an explosion of heavy caliber automatic weapons fire. The windows were blown in, vanishing in a crystal shower of glass. The first big slugs hit Earl square in the chest and flung the big man across the room. He was dead before he stopped moving.

The gunfire was relentless, rips of bullets stitching across the room, raking it with fire. Fields sat frozen in his seat, paralyzed by terror.

"Get down, stupid!" Hall's beefy arm swung, knocking Fields out of his chair, knocking him to the glass-swept floor.

As the gunfire came back for another pass, Relyea overturned the dining table for a little cover. The bullets were chewing up everything, shredding out the walls, shooting out the light in the ceiling. The shooting stopped for a moment only, but somewhere in the house they heard the sound of more glass breaking.

"What's that?" said Hall.

"Someone's breaking in," Relyea said, starting to stand up, but Hall dragged him down.

"What, are you crazy? If that thing opens up again, you'll be cut in half."

"Jesus Christ!" Jimmy Fields gasped. "What's happening?"

The shooting began again, this time it seemed to be even more intense. Relyea and Hall flattened themselves on the floor. They had their guns out now, but they could not raise themselves an inch without getting plugged for sure.

Hall turned and fired a single shot, hitting the last working lamp in the room. Suddenly, they were plunged into darkness. The firing stopped again.

"It's over," said Fields.

"The hell it is," growled Hall. He and Relyea leaned around both sides of the table and started firing back. Fields couldn't help himself. He bolted from between the two cops and started to crawl across the floor on his hands and knees. The machine gun started up again, and the policemen dove for cover.

"Where did Fields go?" Relyea yelled.

"Oh, shit," said Hall. "I have to go get him." He started to crawl away, and when the gunfire stopped, he got to his feet and ran through the house. "Fields?" Hall shouted. "Where the hell are you?"

But there was no answer from Jimmy Fields. Then, out in the night, Hall could make out the sound of a heavy, powerful engine turning over, then roaring away from the beach house.

Relyea was at his side. He carried what appeared to be a bundle of rags in his hands. "What happened?"

"Fields—he's been snatched."

"Oh, shit," said Relyea. "Max is going to be pissed . . ."

Hall looked at the charred cloth Relyea carried. "What the hell is that?"

Relyea held up the fabric. "It used to be my suit coat," he said. "But it got shot . . ."

Hall laughed. "Give it a good burial, Arthur."

"Well," said Relyea. "I got some bad news for you Eddie . . . Yours did not make it, either."

Hoover arrived at the beach house just before dawn, the sun just beginning to peer over the hills. There were lots of cops at the scene, an evidence team was walking every inch of the ground around the house and taking plaster casts of tire marks on the driveway. Every bullet was being extracted from the walls—there were enough slugs to keep ballistics busy for weeks.

Earl still lay where he had fallen, and Hoover walked over to him, the glass crunching under his feet like gravel. He looked down at Earl, his shattered chest a mass of congealed blood.

"Oh, Earl . . ." said Hoover shaking his head. "I'm sorry."

He walked into the next room to Relyea and Hall.

"So?" he asked.

The two policemen looked wan, their faces wearing a layer of five o'clock shadow, their eyes haggard.

"I still feel bad about Earl," said Hall.

"He was dead before he hit the ground," said Relyea, fingering the stubble on his chin.

"Did you see whoever it was who took Fields?" Hoover asked. "Did you get anything?"

"Aww, Jeez, Max, we couldn't see shit," said Hall. "I don't know what kind of gun they had out there, but it was a big one. Some kind of heavy automatic. Look at this place . . ."

"It was like they were trying to shoot down a B-17," said Relyea.

"I think they would liked to have killed us," said Hall; "but if they couldn't, then keeping us on the floor was the next best thing."

"And believe me, they did," Relyea put in.

"They shot the hell out of this place. They had a heavy machine gun, and they blasted away . . . And while they were doing that, the fruitcake got spooked and took a powder."

A uniformed cop leaned into the room. "Lieutenant, they want you down on the beach."

As the four cops clambered down the dunes, they could see a knot of uniforms and evidence cops standing around a body.

"Oh, God," Hoover groaned. "I think we know who that is . . ."

Jimmy Fields looked as if he had been marinated in some kind of caustic solution. His clothes were missing, and his body appeared tattered, as if he had been whipped and beaten.

"He just came in on the tide, Lieutenant," said one of the uniformed cops.

"Where are his clothes?" asked Relyea.

"Can you believe it, the water strips the clothes right off 'em," said Hall, who had seen his fair share of floaters in his time.

Relyea knelt down and lifted Jimmy Field's head. There was a massive bullet wound there.

"Well, we know he didn't drown," said Hoover.

Bobby and Milt, the coroners, looked at

Jimmy Field's mangled body on the slab, then they looked up at Hoover. Both men shrugged.

"What can I tell you, Max . . . They put a gun in his mouth and shot the back of his head off."

"It's known to be fatal," Bobby quipped.

"It was an execution," said Hoover.

"Well," said Bobby. "I think the jury was out for a while . . ."

"What's that supposed to mean?"

"He got messed up pretty bad before he died," Milt explained. "I've got contusions, abrasions, ccc hymoses around the neck . . . and that's just what I can see. Who knows what happened inside. I'd be willing to bet there's a considerable amount of internal damage."

"So, in other words, they beat the shit out of him," said Relyea.

"That would be the technical term," said Bobby, laughing.

"Are you ever serious about anything?" Relyea asked.

Bobby looked around at the corpses parked around the room like a traffic jam. "Hey, what have I got to be glum about?"

"Think he talked?" Hoover asked Relyea.

"No!" said Relyea.

"Were they lovers," Milt asked. "This guy and that girl from the other day?"

Hoover shook his head. "No, Milt. Just friends . . ."

"Milt is such a romantic," said Bobby.

"Shut up, Bobby," said Milt. "I don't give a damn if they were lovers or not. I just wanted to know if they had any contact . . ."

"Why?"

"Well, I checked out that piece of glass in her foot . . ." As he spoke, Milt guided them toward an X ray light box on the wall.

"And?"

"Look—" Milt snapped on the light. "We took these X rays of Allison Pond, and look what happened. There were six or eight transparencies of Allison taken from various angles. Only now could the men see just how horrible the devastation visited Allison's slight body had been. Her bones were in fragments, deep fractures glowed in the middle of strong, thick bones, and bone splinters were scattered throughout her softer tissues. It was all Hoover could do to look at the images.

"Yeah, so?" asked Relyea, studying the X rays intently.

"I shot these before the autopsy, when they first brought her in," said Milt. "She hadn't been touched."

"I still don't get it," said Relyea.

"Look at the feet . . ."

One of the feet was simply not there. In its place was a milky, blurred smudge.

"Gamma rays fogged the film," Milt explained. "That little piece of glass was very radioactive . . ."

16

Morris Tischfeld, haberdasher of distinction, was the tailor of choice for Max Hoover and his cohorts, and they paid a visit to his place of business later that day. To do police business wearing anything other than a sharp, well-tailored suit was something unthinkable.

Morris himself took care of the four policemen. He measured Hall carefully while Relyea went through the racks looking for the right garment. Hoover was sitting in one of the large leather armchairs in the dressing room.

"Is this bulge you or your gun?" Morris asked Hall, prodding him in the chest. "Or are you putting on weight?"

Hall slapped his stomach. "Hell, no, Morris,"

he said. "I'm still the same weight I was the day I got married."

"Which day?" Morris asked. "You've been married five times."

"Just do your job," Hall growled. "I wouldn't be here except some bozos shot my fuckin' suit full of holes."

"Holes from a thirty-five or forty-fives we can mend," said Morris. "Machine-gun holes no can do."

Coolidge was wandering around the store, fingering merchandise. "Why would this guy Timms kill Allison Pond?" he asked suddenly. He picked up a tie and thoughtfully felt the silk between his thumb and forefinger.

The only person in the room not surprised by the naïveté of the question was Morris—who didn't know what Coolidge was talking about.

" Come on, Ellery," said Relyea. "Isn't it obvious."

"Yeah," Hall agreed. "Timms had her knocked off because he was screwing her and she had it on film."

"Yes, I know that," said Coolidge. "But is that reason enough to kill her? I mean, what would really happen if it came out that they were screwing each other? I mean, would *you* care, Max? Would any of us care if some military bureaucrat was fooling around on his wife?''

''No,'' said Hoover. ''We wouldn't care. But his bosses back in Washington would. He'd lose his job, probably get thrown out of the army. His life would be ruined. People have been killed for a lot less.''

''Maybe its worse,'' said Relyea. ''Maybe there's film of the general screwing Jimmy Fields.''

''I'd give a week's pay to see that film,'' said Coolidge. He held a suit coat to his chest, measuring it for size. ''Hey, Morris, what color is this?''

''This is avocado,'' said the tailor. ''A very popular color this season.''

Coolidge turned to Hoover. ''Max, what do you think of this color?''

''I think you can't shoot a man wearing an avocado suit,'' he said, getting to his feet. ''Let's go see Timms.''

Relyea was turning this way and that in front of a triple mirror, modeling his new suit. ''Where is he? Washington?''

''No,'' said Hoover. ''He's in Nevada. Vegas.''

The Buick blasted across the desert on Highway 15, the road flat and straight and empty. The top was down, and the sun hammered them. As a concession to the sun, the four men had removed their jackets, but they kept their fedoras on their heads.

Coolidge had to shout to make himself heard against the wind. "You know, I've been thinking, it's funny . . ."

"Here we go," said Eddie Hall. "Tell us what's on your mind, Ellery."

"Well, you know, I grew up in Jersey and I knew that movies come from Hollywood. But I thought Hollywood was this place with little brown houses and horses tied up in front of them."

Eddie Hall and Max Hoover exchanged quick looks, that expression that says "I have no idea where he's going with this, do you?"

"You know what I mean? You know, like Gene Autry ties Champion outside the sheriff's office. I thought everybody in Hollywood had a horse, because cowboy movies were the only kind I went to . . ."

"If you had only gone to Cagney movies, would you have thought everyone out here was a gangster?" Relyea asked.

"They're not?" said Hall.

"That's beside the point. The point is, I thought everyone had a horse. I wanted to get to California so bad. I wanted that horse."

"And when you finally got to California, did Ellery get his horsie?" Hall asked, his voice full of phony solicitousness.

Ellery Coolidge's enthusiasm for his subject allowed him to ignore the sarcasm. "If you remember, some of the cowboys always tied their horses to the rail carefully. But not Gene Autry. No, Gene Autry would just loop the reins around the pole once, then he'd go right in and see the sheriff."

Relyea stared hard at Coolidge, trying to figure out where this eccentric tale would end up. "And?" he prompted.

"Jesus," said Coolidge laughing. "Did I worry about the horse getting away from Gene."

"That's it?" Eddie Hall asked.

"That's it, funny, huh?"

"Hysterical."

"You know what used to occur to me?" said Relyea.

"Oh, boy," said Hall.

"The guns," Relyea said.

"What about them?"

"Well, you know . . . The Cisco Kid or John Wayne or somebody is walking down the main street of Dodge City. He's got a six-gun in each hand, okay . . ."

"Right," said Coolidge, paying very close attention.

"There are desperadoes all over the place. One comes out of a saloon shooting. Blam! The Cisco Kid drops him. The bad guy goes down, and his gun goes flying. There's a bad guy up on the roof with a rifle. The Cisco Kid swings around and—Blam! Drops him, too. The bad guy falls off the roof, his rifle goes flying . . ."

"Yeah," said Coolidge.

"Well, all these neat guns are just *there*, on the ground. And I'm sitting there wondering, does someone go around and pick them up? Is it finders keepers? Could *I* just pick up one of those guns or is someone going to say 'hey kid, get away from those guns.' "

"Christ," said Hall. "Relyea has caught whatever the hell screwy disease it is that Ellery's got."

"Jeez, Arthur, that's an interesting question," said Coolidge earnestly. "I don't know. Something else for me to worry about. What do you say, Max?"

The Buick roared by a huge billboard on the side of the road. It showed a roulette wheel, a big ace of spades, and a pretty girl playing with a beach ball on the shores of Lake Meade.

"I say welcome to Nevada."

They knew they were near the Atomic Energy Commission test site when they noticed that someone had bothered to fence the desert. The barrier was an elaborate one—a barbed-wire fence some ten feet tall, topped by skeins of murderously sharp razor wire. Any gates they passed were heavily padlocked.

"They seem very worried about someone stealing their desert," said Max Hoover as they drove past miles and miles of fence.

Finally, they found a manned checkpoint, a heavy gate guarded by a stout brick guardhouse. As the Buick rolled to a halt at the gate, a soldier in olive drab fatigues carrying an M-1 rifle emerged and waved the big car to a halt.

Hoover had his badge out, and he let the guard—he couldn't have been more than twenty years old—get a good look at it. "Los Angeles Police Department," he said. "I want to see General Timms."

The guard compared the name on Hoover's identification with a list of names on a clipboard. "You are not on my list or authorized visitors, sir."

"Well, how do I get on that list, Private?"

"I have to get authorization for that, sir."

"Then, get it . . . Tell them this is about a homicide."

The guard took Hoover's badge and ID and entered the guardhouse. He was on the phone for some time.

Up ahead on the access road, they could just make out a cluster of Quonset huts and barracks, barely visible in the glare of the sun.

"Five to one we don't get in," said Hoover.

"This is the army," said Hall nodding. "It never changes."

"I'll take those odds," said Coolidge.

Coolidge lost. The guard returned to the car and handed back his ID folder. "Sorry, sir. No civilian admittance," he said. "There are no exceptions."

"Did you talk to General Timms?"

The guard almost smiled. Privates did not talk to generals unless something had gone very, very wrong or if the private in question has won the Congressional Medal of Honor.

"No, sir, I did not speak to General Timms, sir."

"Then, who did you talk to?"

"I have no information for you, sir, other than to say that the general is unavailable."

Hoover looked beyond the guard to the buildings up the access road. "Did you tell them this was official police business?"

"Yes, sir, I did."

"Did you tell them this was an inquiry about a homicide?"

"Yes, sir, I did," said the soldier. "They said no civilian admittance. No exceptions."

Hoover gave the young man a long hard look. "You plan on making the service your career, son?"

"Yes, sir, I do."

"Then, I predict a great career, for you. You'll make general in no time."

"Well, thank you, sir. Now, if you'll just back up your vehicle . . ."

They drove back onto the highway and passed more long miles of fence.

"Think we could get over that?" Hoover asked.

"Sure," said Eddie Hall. "Trouble is, we'd be dead by the time we got to the other side. There's no way I'm going near that razor wire."

"Could we ram it?"

Relyea spoke this time. "The fence posts are made of concrete, and they're probably buried deep.

"So lets not try to ram it," said Coolidge.

Suddenly, Hoover stood on the brakes, and the Buick screeched to a halt on the hot highway. He slammed the car into reverse and backed up fast.

"Well, looky here," he said.

It was a gate, padlocked, but unattended. And beyond that a dirt road leading into the testing range. Relyea was the first out of the car, his gun out of its holster. He aimed it at the lock and was about to pull the trigger when Hall stopped him.

"Wait a minute!"

Eddie Hall got out of the car. "What is this? Amateur hour? Arthur, you know what'll happen when your bullet hits that padlock?"

"It'll break?"

"You've been watching too many movies, you and your fruit loop friend in the backseat," said Hall. "You shoot at that, your bullet will be coming straight back at you."

"It always works in the movies," said Relyea.

"Sure," said Hall, digging his wallet out of his back pocket. "And in the movies crime doesn't pay, either . . ." He pulled a lock pick from one of the crevasses in the wallet. "Whereas we know in real life that crime pays very well."

"Yeah . . . yeah . . ." said Relyea.

Hall squinted at the lock and then went to work with his pick. Ten minutes later he was still working, and the lock remained willfully locked.

Hoover looked at his watch every ten seconds or so. Coolidge sweated buckets in the hot sun. Relyea just stared into space, lost in thought.

The pick got slippery in Hall's sweaty fingers, and he dropped it more than once. "Damn it!" He picked up the instrument and went back to it.

Hoover waited another minute, then stepped

up to the gate. "Come on, Eddie," he said. "Let me try."

"Hey," said Hall. "I almost got it."

"No you haven't." He took out his gun and put a single slug into the mechanism. The lock shattered.

"There," said Hoover. "Let's go."

The soft suspension of the Buick was not built for dirt roads, and the big car bounced and jolted along a rough track designed for the tougher springs of military vehicles. The land on the other side of the fence was considerably different from the open desert. The earth was darker than the desert, with an almost shiny quality to the soil, and it was barren of any living thing.

Up ahead, sprawled across the road were bodies, dozens of them, men, women, and children . . .

Hoover stopped the car, and the four men tumbled out. The bodies were not bodies at all, but department store mannequins, strewn around for hundreds of yards—armless, headless, and naked.

Beyond them was a vast crater, hundreds of yards across. The men approached the edge of the chasm and peered down into it. The effect of this immense void was unsettling.

"Jesus," said Hoover. "That is one giant fuckin' hole."

"They just drop it there," said Hall.

"That's what happens after they set one off at ground level," said Relyea. "You get a big hole. Did you know that before they drop the bomb, they have to carve a big X marks the spot in the desert? Its something like a hundred yards across and six feet deep. Then a plane goes up with a bomb and tries to hit it."

"Now, that's a great way to earn a living," said Hall. "Digging a big X in the desert so some clown can blow it up."

Coolidge looked to the clear blue sky, trying to imagine the towering mushroom cloud.

"Where's all the dirt?"

"Vaporized with everything else," said Relyea. "It's dust."

"What happens if they set one off while we're here?" said Coolidge a trifle uneasily.

"Then *we're* dust," said Hall.

Coolidge looked to the horizon as if he could see an atom bomb being lobbed at them. Instead, he saw something else. A vehicle was roaring toward them, kicking up the sand.

"Uh-oh," said Coolidge. "We got company."

"Time to go, Max?" Hall asked.

Hoover nodded. "Time to go, Eddie."

The four men raced for the Buick.

17

The Buick shot down the dusty track, the fat whitewalls throwing up a high wake of sand, the car lumbered hard and foundered on the track. Only the weight of the car kept it on track.

The military vehicle in pursuit of the four cops was some kind of souped-up half-track, the treads designed to run on sand as if it was smooth blacktop. It was gaining on them fast, but the gate was just over the next rise. Hoover assumed that once they were on asphalt, the Buick could really open up and bury the army.

But things wouldn't quite unfold that way. They had the gate in sight, and there were three eight-ton military four-by-four trucks and a jeep.

"Oh, shit!" said Hoover. "I think we're about to become POWs, guys."

There seemed to be soldiers everywhere, three full squads. Every single one of them had a rifle, and every one was pointed at Hoover and his men.

"Hands up!" a master sergeant roared. "Get outta the car!"

The sand half-track pulled up behind the Buick, the fifty-caliber machine gun was cocked and aimed. There was no possibility of escape.

As Hoover got out of the car, he stared at the jeep. The man in charge, a full colonel, sat in the front passenger seat, with a captain-adjutant in the back. The colonel was looking at Hoover with undisguised hatred. Three men in silver protective suits came forward, their heads sheathed in helmets with plastic windows. The men moved slowly, as if the suits were very heavy. They passed Geiger counters over the car and over the four men, then examined the readings on their detection meters.

"They're clean, sir," one of the technicians shouted, his voice muffled inside his helmet.

For a long moment no one moved. Then the colonel, who was sitting in one of the trucks, walked toward the four men. He held a part of the ruined padlock in his right hand.

Hoover read the name tape on the colonel's uniform. He was Colonel Fitzgerald. He looked at Hoover and then at the other three—his look of loathing replaced with a sort of cold disdain.

When he spoke, he was formal, all buisness. "You men are in violation of federal law," he said. "This is a restricted government installation. I could have all of you shot." He looked directly at Hoover. "Do you have some form of identification?"

Fitzgerald took his time examining Hoover's badge and card. "Lieutenant Hoover . . . Los Angeles Police Department?"

"We're investigating a homicide," said Hoover.

"I don't care if you're looking for Jack the Ripper," said Fitzgerald. "But you are way outside your jurisdiction, Lieutenant. Are you aware of the penalties for trespassing on a federally restricted area." He held up the broken lock. "And the penalties for destroying government property?"

"We go where the case takes us," said Hoover, his eyes locking onto Fitzgerald's, defiant, holding his gaze.

Fitzgerald did not like these men in their flashy clothes and with their air of studied nonchalance. They thought they were tough guys, sophisticated men wise to the ways of the world and the underworld. But Fitzgerald saw nothing more than cheap cops—thugs recruited to keep in line other thugs—and kept in line themselves with a measure of authority and a bright, gaudy automobile.

"Not if it takes you here, you don't," said Fitzgerald. "Out here it's military law, and I'm in charge of enforcing it." He turned to his adjutant. "Captain, escort these men to the base and lock them up."

"Yes, sir." As the captain and some of his men moved toward Hoover and his crew, the field telephone in the half-track buzzed.

"Colonel?" said a corporal, holding the receiver out to Fitzgerald. "The general for you, sir."

With a certain reluctance, Fitzgerald took the phone. "Yes, sir . . . Yes, sir. We found them on the perimeter, sir, and they had seriously violated security . . ." Fitzgerald was silent a moment as Timms spoke. No one else could hear the general's words, but it was obvious that Colonel Fitzgerald did not care in the least for what Timms was saying. He grimaced, then scowled.

"If I may say so, sir, I'm not sure that's a good idea. No . . . Yes, sir . . . Yes, sir. As ordered. Yes, sir." He hung up, frowned, and pointed at Hoover.

"Put that one in the jeep," the colonel ordered. "Take the rest of them to the base lockup. They can wait there."

"When do we get Hoover back?" asked Coolidge.

"When I decide," snapped Colonel Fitzgerald. "And if I see this car in a restricted area again, I'll burn it. And I'll burn anyone who'll have the misfortune to be in it."

The general may have lived on an army base in the middle of a desert, but that was no reason to live in discomfort. The Atomic Energy Commission had built a very handsome house for the general; a modern, low-slung, glass and sandstone building, set in the middle of an acre of lush green grass—a man-made oasis of grass irrigated at vast expense to the American taxpayer. Near the house was a stable, and as the jeep carrying Hoover pulled up, an orderly walked a beautiful black stallion out into the sun and started to currycomb the animal's gleaming flanks.

"You know," said Hoover. "When I was in the service, it wasn't like this at all. Things have changed."

"Shut your mouth and follow me," said Colonel Fitzgerald, leading the way into the house.

The interior of the house was icy with air-conditioning, a chilly, but pleasant, shock after the scorching desert air. Hoover drank the cool air like cold beer. The house was immaculately kept and tastefully furnished in the spare wood and leather Scandinavian furniture that was beginning to be popular on the American side of the Atlantic.

"Take him to the study," Colonel Fitzgerald ordered the captain. "And keep him there."

"Yes, sir."

The den was wood-paneled and had a large picture window that looked out to the desert and the mountains beyond. There was an extravagantly large desk with three separate telephones and a table bearing an impressive array of liquors.

"Don't mind if I do," said Hoover. He dropped a couple of ice cubes from the silver ice bucket into a crystal glass and poured some twelve-year-old scotch over them. He sipped and savored the smoky smoothness of the alcohol on his tongue.

"Hey, Captain," he said to his jailer. "You should have some of this. This is the good stuff."

"Why don't you pipe down?"

Hoover shrugged. "I'm just being friendly . . ." Hoover started examining the room. There was a flagstone fireplace in the middle of one wall. "So, what does the general do? Does he really crank up the air-conditioning, then build himself a nice cozy fire?"

"It gets cold in the desert at night," said the captain.

Hoover took a sip of his drink. "You know, I've heard that before. But I've never believed it."

The captain shrugged. "Suit yourself."

Hoover continued to wander around the room, stopping in front of a case of rifles. Some were antique, others were expensive sporting guns by Holland and Purdeys, more work of art than weapons with their engraved metalwork and hand-carved stocks. The captain knew that the weapons were not loaded and that the case was locked, but he tensed when Hoover got near them.

"Why don't you step away from the weapons, Lieutenant," said the captain. "Just to make me feel better . . ."

"Afraid I'm going to try something?"

"I'm afriad you might try something stupid." He put his hand on the big Colt 45 automatic side arm he wore strapped to his leg. "Something you might come to regret."

"I'm not going to kill you Captain," said Hoover.

"I know," said the captain.

Hoover shrugged again. "Well, if it'll make

you feel better . . ." he said affably and turned his attention to a wall of photographs. The pictures were a Who's Who of movers and shakers in the American military, politics, and scientific community. There were photos of Timms with General Omar Bradley, with Douglas MacArthur, with Eisenhower in his military uniform, and another with Eisenhower as President; there was Timms with President Truman and a picture of a much younger Timms, shaking the hand of Franklin D. Roosevelt. There was even a picture of the general with Albert Einstein, the placid campus of Princeton University in the background.

These familiar faces Hoover recognized, but there were other pictures showing Timms with men Max could not identify.

"Who are these guys?" Hoover asked.

"Edward Teller, Niels Bohr, Enrico Fermi, Robert Oppenheimer," said the captain.

"Are they generals or politicians?"

The captain shook his head, as if pitying Hoover in his ignorance. "They're the greatest scientific minds since Isaac Newton," he said. "Together, they built the atomic bomb."

"Never heard of them," said Hoover slowly.

Beneath the pictures of the general with the famous were aerial views of nuclear explosions, huge balls of fire photographed with some kind high-resolution camera. Hoover bent down and squinted at one of them. In one there were tiny figures, far enough from the explosion to avoid being vaporized, but close enough for them to be washed over with the radioactive mist that blew out in a vast circle from the detonation point.

"What are those?" said Hoover. "People? They're playing it sort of close there, aren't they?"

"Don't worry about it," said the captain. "We know what we're doing."

"I hope so."

"Lieutenant Hoover?"

The captain snapped to attention as General Timms entered the room, Fitzgerald trailing behind him.

"Lieutenant Hoover," said Timms. "I'm General Timms. What can I do for the Los Angeles Police Department?" He turned to the captain still taut at attention. "As you were, Captain."

"Sir," he said, and left the room, closing the door behind him.

18

General Timms looked pale, his face drawn, and he was much thinner than the man in the pictures. He walked stiffly, as if in pain, and he grimaced as he lowered himself into an Eames chair.

"I came to talk about Allison Pond," said Hoover.

The general nodded. "I know . . . Colonel Fitzgerald has informed me." He shifted slightly in the leather chair and pain clouded his features once again.

"Are you okay?" Hoover asked.

"I had a slight riding accident," said Timms. "I pinched a sciatic nerve." He smiled. "Have you ever had back problems, Lieutenant Hoover?"

"I got shot in the back once," he said. He glanced at Fitzgerald as he spoke, as if trying to push the man out of the room with his eyes.

"If I might cut through the formalities, Lieutenant . . . You are aware that Miss Pond and I had a certain relationship.

"Yes, I am."

"And you are aware that she had similar relationships with other men as well as with myself?" His voice was calm, without emotion, as if he was briefing a roomful of junior officers on some arcane point of military order or physics rather than about a beautiful young woman who had loved him once.

Hoover took longer to nod this time. He wondered if the general knew that he was facing one of those men.

"It was a terrible waste," said Timms, as if Allison was not a human being but a precious natural resource that had been thoughtlessly squandered.

"I believe Miss Pond was in your company from Friday through the weekend, is that correct?" Hoover found it difficult to pronounce her name.

Timms shot a quick glance at Fitgerald. "That sounds about right. We flew up to Lake Tahoe on Saturday, I don't remember the exact time.

It was mid-morning. The transport office would have a log with the exact time of departure."

"Wait a minute," said Hoover, taken by surprise. "You were up in Tahoe? You weren't here?"

Timms shook his head. "Senator Boulton has a weekend house that he lends us from time to time."

"Look, General, I know for a fact she was here," said Hoover angrily. "Don't try to fool me. You're just wasting your time."

"I am doing nothing of the sort," said the general patiently, closing his eyes for a moment as if he was a teacher trying to explain a very simple theorem to a very dense student. "We spent Friday evening here, and then we went to Lake Tahoe. And Sunday night I flew to Washington."

Hoover's eyes narrowed. "You're telling me she wasn't out at the test site?"

Timms smiled. "Of course not. It's restricted—but then you know that, don't you, Lieutenant." Timms paused and sighed. "She went back to Los Angeles, Lieutenant Hoover, and I went to Washington for a meeting with the secretary of defense. There should be a record of *that* in the transport office log as well, if you care to look it up."

Timms paused again, as if there was nothing

more to say about the matter of Allison Pond. "Tell me, would you happen to think much about national security, Lieutenant?"

Hoover shook his head. "No, General Timms, I've got all the security problems I can handle in Los Angeles."

"How about atomic energy, Lieutenant?" the general asked. "Ever think about that? Ever think about what it means?"

Hoover was not interested in atomic energy. "All I really know about it is that we dropped two bombs, and presto-change-o, the war was over. I think that's a good thing. I'm glad *we* have it. I'm glad we did the dropping."

Timms smiled, as if at a child's naïveté. "But the physics of, Lieutenant, do you know anything about that? For example, did you know that the atom itself is largely made up of empty space?"

"I never really thought about it," said Hoover shrugging. "I wasn't big on science in school."

"Almost completely empty," Timms continued, "with the exception of tiny fragments of matter. And since the entire universe is made of atoms, everything we see and touch, the very floor we're standing on, is made up of empty space."

"Yes? So what?"

"The only reason we don't fall through it is

that those tiny bits of matter are whirling about at such speed, they give the illusion of solidity," the general went on with his professorial air. "The floor is actually spinning under us, Lieutenant. Can you feel it?"

He looked down. Hoover and Fitzgerald looked down, too, and the general smiled as if he had just pulled off some neat little parlor trick.

"Then, we're just empty space ourselves," said Hoover.

Timms beamed as if he had finally made his thick-witted student see the light. "Exactly! And yet those bits of matter—which are so small no one has ever seen them, not even with the most powerful microscopes, whose existence we can infer only by theory and experiments that seem to confirm the theory—those minute specks of nothingness contain enough energy to destroy this building, the entire city, every person on earth. It's inconceivable, isn't it?"

Hoover got the impression that were it not for the general's back trouble, he would have leaped out of his chair and capered with delight at the power of the tiny bits of matter.

"I don't think much about those things, General," he said softly. "I probably see too much . . ."

"But you see things that have no purpose,"

said Timms dismissively. "These things have no greater significance."

"They're people dead before their time," said Hoover. "That has a certain significance to them."

Fitzgerald looked as if he was about to intervene and end this meeting right then, but Timms sensed this and waved him off.

"It's the history of the world, Lieutenant," said Timms. "People die before their time so others can live. It's the cornerstone of civilization—war, religion, democracy . . . a hundred die so that a thousand may live."

"I don't deal in those numbers. I take 'em one at a time, General Timms," said Hoover. It was obvious that he did not buy the general's grand words. "Right now I've got Allison Pond."

But Timms seemed anxious to win Hoover to his side of the argument. He started to lean forward in his chair again, but the discomfort restrained him as if he was caught in a web of pain.

"Certain men—a doctor, a national leader, an officer of the law—give to society in many ways most people do not, and in return, we give those leaders a certain consideration."

"We do?" Hoover asked.

Timms nodded. "We don't teach it in school,

but those who accept the burden of leadership understand all about it. You know what I mean. You've accepted leadership, haven't you, Lieutenant?''

"In what sense?" Hoover didn't mention that he always felt as if he and his team were always playing catch-up.

"You protect society, you protect the ordinary citizen. And in doing so, perhaps sometimes you break the law, ignore the Constitution, the Bill of Rights, the laws governing search and seizure, illegal imprisonment . . ."

Hoover shrugged. He wasn't going to admit to anything, but it was as if the general had been right there in the Buick, riding with his team day in, day out for a year or more.

"Perhaps it's known that you do this, yet is understood that this is a burden of leadership. And you accept it. You accept your own sins."

Hoover looked like a man who was not too sure he wanted to accept his own sins. From the breast pocket of his suit jacket he pulled out a clean white handkerchief and emptied two small shards of glass onto the table in front of him.

"Allison Pond was at your test site, General," Hoover said. "We found pieces of this in her foot."

Fitzgerald glanced sharply at Timms, who simply smiled at Hoover and shrugged lightly.

"I'm going to need your appointments calendar for the last month, sir," said Hoover. "Where you were, who you saw . . ."

"Of course, you'll have anything you need," said Timms. "Colonel Fitzgerald will attend to anything you request."

Hoover rose. "Thank you. Nice house."

Even though Max had left the room, Fitzgerald felt he had to whisper. "I've spoken to Los Angeles. We'll have it in twenty-four hours."

Hoover was silent for a long time on the drive back to Los Angeles. The nose of the Buick was pointed west, into the setting sun. The desert seemed to glow red as dusk emerged from daylight.

Eddie Hall finally had to ask what had happened during his encounter with General Timms. "So?"

Hoover still looked straight forward. "So what?"

"So what did the general say?"

"He said the cornerstone of civilization was human sacrifice, Eddie."

"That's kinda tough on Allison Pond . . ." said Hall.

19

When Max Hoover and the rest of the team got to the station the next morning, the first person they saw was Esther Newburg.

"Oh, hell, Esther," Hoover said, his shoulders slumping. "It's gonna be one of those days isn't it? You've got your bad-news face on."

Esther Newburg nodded. "Bingo, Max," she rasped. "The chief wants to see you right away."

The chief of police was sitting behind his desk when Hoover was ushered in by the chief's secretary. That was as it should be. It was the man sitting across from the chief that made Hoover's face fall. Max knew a fed when he saw one—and he had seen too many. They all looked more or less alike. Hoover—J. Edgar, that is—recruited agents of a certain type. Ex-servicemen, clean-cut family men, college boys. Irish Catholic was a definite plus.

"Max," said the chief. "I want you to meet Special Agent Jeffrey McCafferty. He's with the FBI."

Max and McCafferty shook hands. The special agent wore the giant school ring of Notre Dame.

"Good to meet you, Hoover," said McCafferty.

"Likewise," Hoover lied.

"Special Agent McCafferty is interested in one of our cases, Max. I told him you were the man to talk to about it."

"That a fact? Which one?"

"Allison Pond," said the chief. "Is that the girl's name, Special Agent?"

McCafferty nodded. "That's the one." The fed knew that neither the chief nor Hoover liked him or wanted him there—the chief was better at hiding it—but McCafferty refused to be drawn.

"Excuse me, Chief," said Hoover. "Would you mind if I inquire what business is this of the FBI's."

McCafferty spoke up before the chief had a chance to answer. "If I may, Chief . . ." He turned to Hoover and flashed him a Pepsodent smile. "The bureau's role here is purely informational, Max. We are aware that a man of fundamental importance to the national security has been brought somehow into the investigation of a young woman's death."

"So?" said Max. "She's dead, and I want to know why."

"Steady, Max," the chief cautioned.

"In light of the damage that such an investigation could do—not only to that man's reputation but to his vital work—the director thought it was appropriate, without stepping on your jurisdiction, of course, to come by informally and share our knowledge of the matter." McCafferty smiled. "See, Max, you're still on the case. Nothing to worry about there."

Hoover was cold. "Knowledge of this case? And what would that be?"

McCafferty leaned forward, earnest and genial. "I am prepared to give you the director's personal guarantee that General Timms had nothing to do with the death of Allison Pond."

Hoover looked at the chief and then back at McCafferty. "And just how would the director know something like that?"

McCafferty smiled a knowing smile. "I am sorry, but I am not at liberty to discuss that."

Hoover waited for McCafferty to continue, but it appeared that he had said all he had to say.

"That's it?" Hoover asked.

The chief looked a little nonplussed himself. "Is that it?"

Hoover leaned forward and scowled. "If I call your boss in Washington, he'll vouch for this pile of crap you're handing us?"

McCafferty kept his temper as Hoover's started to slip away. "The director asked me specifically to say he appreciates your cooperation, Lieutenant Hoover. He is sure you understand the sensitive nature of the situation . . ." McCafferty was still smiling his affable smile when he added: ". . . You being a married man yourself."

Hoover had gone gray with anger. The chief shifted uncomfortably and tried to control his own anger. He hated having a fed come in here and threaten one of his own men. McCafferty never broke a sweat.

"We are not without our resources," McCafferty continued smoothly. "We would be more than happy to share them with you, Lieutenant."

"Thanks," said Hoover through clenched teeth.

"And, Chief, if you should happen to come across anything else in this regard, any *evidence* . . . the director would be grateful to see it for himself . . . The director would be *very* grateful . . ."

McCafferty stood and smiled one more time. "Good morning, gentlemen. And thank you for your cooperation. I know I can count on it . . ."

It was the most subtle of threats, but it carried a potent hazard. He was saying, Don't Cross J. Edgar Hoover . . .

When the special agent had left the room, the chief pounded his fist against the desk. "Damnit, Max. You know how I feel about those snot-nose Ivy League cops being in my town, much less sitting in that chair, let alone in my office."

"Yes, sir. I do."

"That damn Hoover! Eisenhower ought to fire him. I can't wait till he's gone for good." The chief jabbed a cigarette into his mouth and lit it. "Do you have anything hard on this guy Timms?"

Hoover shook his head. "He's lying about Allison Pond. And you can take it to the bank . . . But not yet."

"You can't prove it?"

"Not yet," said Hoover. "But I will. Jesus, Bill, we had an informant killed along with Earl. They hit them with a heavy caliber machine gun. It's military . . . That's the connection."

The chief sat back in his tall leather chair.

"What the hell are you talking about, Max? You're tying in the whole goddamn United States Army because of some damn weapon? I know three guys one block of Lankershim in North Hollywood with that ordnance in their back rooms. Wake up, for Christ's sake."

The two men glared at one another for a long moment. Then Hoover spoke, his voice low and slow. "When we set this thing up, Bill, the understanding was that we answered to no one but you. That was the deal. Four men, no politics, no favors for anybody, we answer to nobody . . ."

"When we set this thing up, Max, it was to go after criminals and gangsters," the chief said angrily. "I didn't ask you four to go after the goddamn Atomic Energy Commission."

"What if they're killing people, Bill?" Hoover asked. "What if they're killing people as sure as some thug in an alley? Or some wise guy selling bad junk? I don't see the difference."

"You're being naive, Max. That's not like you at all."

Hoover smacked his fist on the desk. "You know I'm right, Bill."

"Right?" the chief asked. "You know, there's a lot of people you fellas took for a ride or went to talk to, and no one's seen them since.

Nobody looked into that too carefully. I wonder how right that is?"

Hoover's voice was quieter, softer. "Allison Pond never hurt anybody, Bill. Except herself . . ."

The chief shook his head and seemed to pity him. "Maxwell, listen to yourself. She must have hurt somebody. Or we wouldn't be talking about her like this. We wouldn't be talking about her in the past tense . . ."

Katherine Hoover was just on her way out when there was an insistent knocking at the front door. She opened it to find Jeffrey McCafferty and two other agents standing on her doorstep. McCafferty's affable, ingratiating smile was gone, replaced with a stony mask.

Unlike her husband, Katherine Hoover did not know how to spot a fed when she saw one.

"Yes," she said. "May I help you?"

"Mrs. Hoover?" he said, flashing his badge. "FBI. I have a warrant to search the premises."

It took a few seconds for the information to sink in. "Excuse me? I'm sorry?" The other two agents eased past her and entered the house.

"Warrant, Mrs. Hoover." He thrust a piece of paper into her hands and pushed by her roughly.

"A warrant?" She looked at the document,

but the words refused to make sense under her eyes. She turned and ran into the house, chasing after the agents. "What is this all about? Please tell me."

"You can make this nice and easy, Mrs. Hoover," said McCafferty. He was standing in the middle of the Hoover living room, looking around like a general surveying a battlefield. "You just tell me where the film is, we won't touch a thing and we'll be on our way."

"Film? said Katherine. "What kind of film?"

McCafferty sighed. "Okay, Mrs. Hoover, if that's the way you want to play it. Mike, start with the bookcases."

The agent crossed the room and started sweeping the books from the shelves. McCafferty and his colleague went farther into the house. Katherine followed them into the master bedroom.

"Please, please . . . This is some kind of mistake. My husband is a policeman, for God's sake."

"Oh, we know that, Mrs. Hoover."

"I'm calling him right now," said Katherine, grabbing the phone next to the bed. She dialed quickly. "Esther, it's Katherine. Get Max! Get him now!"

The agent was stripping the sheets from the bed. "There's nothing under here, Jeff."

"Cut the mattress open."

The agent produced a large pocketknife and thrust it into the mattress. "No! No! Please!" Katherine screamed. It was as if someone was cutting into the very heart of her marriage.

20

Max wasn't in the office; he was in a bar. Along with Relyea and Hall, both with their arms around pretty girls they had picked up somewhere, Coolidge and Max were wedged into a booth of a club on Sunset. The two women were fascinated by the fact that their companions were police officers.

"You guys are a lot different than those guys on *Dragnet*," said the blond one. "Those guys don't look like they'd be any fun at all."

"*Dragnet*," said Eddie Hall. "That stuff ain't real."

"Cops don't talk like that," said Relyea.

"Yeah, said Coolidge. He swung into his patented Jack Web imitation. "Nine-forty-five— went to the refrigerator—wanted ham and cheese sandwich," he deadpanned. "Couldn't find the mayonnaise, so I found the mustard instead. Nobody talks like that."

"Da-da-da-da." Relyea sang the *Dragnet* signature music.

"Feds," said Hoover in disgust, staring into his drink.

The partners exchanged looks. They hadn't asked Hoover what went on in the chief's office. As always, they knew he would tell them when he was good and ready to tell them.

"Timms called the FBI, and they got to the chief," said Hoover. "One of them was there when I went in."

"Oh, shit," said Hall.

"They want the film," said Hoover. "That's all they're interested in. They don't give a shit about the girl."

The two girls at the table exchanged looks. Suddenly, these guys weren't all that much fun to be with.

"Well," said the brunet, "We have to run."

"Thanks for the drinks, guys," said the blond as they skittered off, unsteady on their high heels.

Neither Hall nor Relyea protested this hasty exit. Instead, they signaled a waiter for another round of drinks.

"They mentioned the film?" said Hall. "They

actually said they wanted it? They know for sure that it exists."

"Not in so many words," said Hoover, draining his glass of scotch. "But he mentioned evidence. That's what he meant."

"How did they know we had it?"

Relyea shrugged. "It must have been Jimmy Fields. They beat him until he told them about it."

"Well, be careful," said Hoover, standing up. "You know what happens next, don't you?"

"What?" Ellery Coolidge asked.

"They come after us . . ."

When Hoover pulled the Buick into the driveway, he noticed at once that all the lights were on in his house and that the front door had been thrown open, a box of light lying across the front lawn.

He got out of the car and ran across the lawn, running through the flower beds and into the house. Kay was sitting in the living room, her eyes closed, as if she could not stand to look at her devastated home. Tears seeped from under her lids and rolled down her cheeks. Hoover could see that she had begun to put the room back together, then stopped, overwhelmed by the havoc. He took her in his arms and hugged her.

"Kay? Are you hurt?"

"No," she whispered. He looked over her shoulder at the wreckage. The room had been turned over just as thoroughly as the apartments of Jimmy Fields and Allison Pond. Slipcovers had been yanked from upholstered pieces of furniture, the contents of every drawer dumped on the floor. Beyond the living room he could see similar ruin in the kitchen.

"What happened?" he whispered in her ear.

"The FBI was here," said Katherine. "They had a search warrant, and they said they were here for the film."

Hoover nodded and started for the steps that ran down to the basement. The door was hanging half off its hinges, and the basement had been tossed, too. Hoover knelt in the middle of the basement and removed a false panel and reached into the small hole, retrieving a can of film. The film was still there.

"Max," said Katherine, her voice high and tight. "You have to tell me what is going on."

He spoke as he replaced the film and hid it. "The man in the film is named Thomas Timms," he said quickly. "He is the head of the Atomic Energy Commission. That means he has powerful friends."

"I don't understand."

"The girl is dead."

"And that's all?"

Hoover stood and walked for the steps. "That's all."

Her frustration bubbled over. "Max, damn it!" she yelled at her husband's back. "Stop being the cop with me . . ."

"You know," said McCafferty to his two agents, "their jurisdiction ends at the county line. You know why these guys are Los Angeles PD? Because they couldn't make the grade. Warrants, wiretaps . . . These gorillas barely know how to read one, never mind know how to apply for one . . ."

It had been a very satisfying workday for the three agents, but it was getting late and they wanted to get home. McCafferty led them into the parking garage beneath the Los Angeles Federal building.

"Follow proper procedure," McCafferty continued as he felt in his pocket for his car keys. "Follow proper procedures and you cannot fail boys. Mister John Edgar himself told me that." They stopped in front of McCafferty's car, a nice, plain Ford. An FBI kind of car.

"That prick on the LAPD thinks he got it over on me, so I fix his ass. I get a search warrant on his premises."

"What would you do if Hoover showed up

here?'' said Mike, looking around the garage, peering into dim corners.

"Mr. Hoover or that dick on the LAPD?"

"Which one do you think I mean?" said Mc-Cafferty laughing. "If Hoover shows up here, I'll arrest him for trespassing."

While they were laughing, Max Hoover stepped out of the darkness and swung his sap, smashing it into the back of Mike's skull. He closed up like a folding chair and collapsed, as the two startled men turned, Hoover swung the sap again, putting out the lights of the other agent.

"Hoover . . . !" gasped McCafferty.

Max landed a quick, hard kick to McCafferty's groin, as he doubled over in pain, Hoover turned his attention back to the second agent. He grabbed a handful of the unlucky man's hair and slammed him headfirst into the side window of McCafferty's Ford. The glass cracked under the force of impact, and the agent bounced off the glass and collapsed unconscious to the concrete.

McCafferty groaned and tried to put some steel in his rubbery legs. Hoover smacked him twice in the face, light, taunting bitch slaps, then started shoving him out of the garage and into the street. He booted him hard in the ass, and

McCafferty fell forward and rolled down the ramp into the gutter.

As he tried to rise, Hoover punched him again, but hard this time, a real start-at-the-floor uppercut. It cracked right on target, the point bone of his chin, and pyrotechnics exploded behind his eyes. He went down again.

Hoover looked blurred as he stood over him, but Special Agent McCafferty heard every word the policeman uttered.

"See, in there, in the garage, that was federal property," Hoover said. "But out here in the street, this isn't. Out here its Los Angeles. This is my town. Out here, you're the trespasser."

For a moment it seemed as if McCafferty was going to pass out, so Hoover slapped him to keep him conscious.

"Hey, listen to me . . . Out here, I can pick you up, burn your house, fuck your wife, and kill your dog. There's only one thing you can do to protect yourself, and that's get out of town. If I can't find you, I can't hurt you. But you're unlucky McCafferty. I already found you."

Hoover bent down and picked the man up by the lapels and started dragging him toward the Buick. "Come on," he said. "I want to show you something."

McCafferty felt fear shoot through his pain.

"What are you doing?" he managed to say. "Where are you taking me?"

"Don't worry, Special Agent," said Hoover. "I'm just taking you to see a local beauty spot."

"Wha . . . ?" said McCafferty.

"You're going to see the world-famous Mulholland Falls . . ."

21

When there was a knock at the door of the Hoover house the next morning, Katherine recoiled, full of fear that they had come back. Max had returned home late the night before, the skin on the knuckles of his right hand broken and raw. They both knew she didn't believe the excuse he gave, something about falling down in a parking lot somewhere. She knew her husband well—she would not be surprised if he had been out roaming the dark city looking to exact some measure of revenge.

She decided not to answer the door—then she immediately changed her mind. Katherine squared her shoulders and forced herself into the hallway. She could not go through life terrified at every knock at the door.

Opening the door an inch, she saw that there was no one standing on the front porch. With great caution she stepped out into the doorway and looked down.

The package was about a foot long, wrapped with brown paper and tied securely with twine. Her name—Mrs. Maxwell Hoover—was printed in block letters across the front. She gazed down at it for a moment, telling herself to leave it there, to run away from it, but her curiosity began torturing her instantly. Maybe there was something in that package that could help, that could clear up the mess their lives had become . . .

Quickly, she knelt, grabbed the package, and darted back into the safety of her home, closing the door and bolting it firmly.

Max Hoover made a point of getting home early and sober that night, pulling the Buick in behind his wife's car, a pert little Nash Metropolitan. He was glad to see that his wife was home.

Hoover felt sorry for his wife. It was never easy to be married to a cop, and it was even harder if that cop happened to be Maxwell Hoover. The guilt he felt was caustic, corrosive. He felt guilty about the hell he had put Katherine through—not just in the last few days, but throughout the course of the marriage—and he felt guilty about the fact that she had taken it, accepting his moods, his hours, his eccentric way of living with hardly a word of complaint.

It wasn't that she was a doormat, a woman frightened of being alone, putting up with an unreasonable man just so she could say she *had* a man. Rather, he knew that she was being strong for both of them, capable and resolute through the stormy season of married life, through the small summer squalls about trivial things to roaring northeasters over the major themes of marriages—sex, money, family, fidelity. It was her way of showing her commitment to him, to his work, to their shared life.

Mostly, he felt guilty about Allison Pond. He was full of remorse at having betrayed his wife, guilty for loving the woman he had broken faith with. He was heavyhearted by the death of one of the women he loved.

Max Hoover got out of the car, bone-weary, but remembered, despite his fatigue, not to walk through the flower beds.

Katherine was not waiting at the door, like a little wifey for her man to come home. But that didn't surprise him; she never was. But she wasn't in the living room, the kitchen, or the bedroom, either.

"Kay?" he called. But his voice seemed to make the house seem even more empty, even more still. Then he noticed the door to the basement stairs was open, and he could hear the faint whir of the electric motor in the movie projector downstairs in the cellar.

Katherine was sitting on the floor, her back against the wall. The brown paper wrapper and the empty film can were there on the concrete next to her. The only light came from the screen.

Hoover and Allison Pond were there, the film shot in the bedroom of her Los Feliz apartment. She was kneeling beside the bed, Hoover was on top of her and taking her from behind, working his penis in and out, slamming her hard. His eyes were closed, and his intense pleasure was obvious.

Hoover felt his heart sink and a look of profound sadness crossed his features. He realized that they had finally attained that telling, crystalline moment in their lives, that moment that passes in an instant, but after which everything is changed irrevocably.

Katherine did not turn toward him, but continued to gaze at the images on the movie screen.

"How long did it last, Max?" she asked. Her voice sounded hollow yet slick with tears.

"Six months," he said softly. "A little less . . ."

"Did everyone know? Were people laughing at me, or pitying me, while I knew nothing?"

"Nobody knew," said Hoover.

She continued to watch the film mesmerized. On the screen his other self, a different man, continued to buck and strain holding Allison tight as he stopped paralyzed by his orgasm. He dropped his cheek against her back, tenderly kissing her spine as he held her close. The delicacy and the affection of those soft kisses, cut deep into Katherine's heart; they seemed more of a betrayal than the animal rutting that had preceded it.

"It's been over a long time," said Hoover, realizing as he spoke the words how empty and futile they sounded.

She turned and looked at him, the tears on her face glinting in the harsh light, then got to her feet and walked out of the room. He did not reach for her as she passed, and he welcomed her stinging slap as it slashed across his face, the commencement of his punishment.

He sat at the kitchen table, a bottle and a glass in front of him. Hoover knew the drill—he was supposed to get drunk; it was what was required of him, but he didn't want a drink, the liquor burned hot and bruising on his tongue. He was pouring himself another when the phone rang. Lifting the receiver, he held it to his ear but did not speak at once.

"Hoover?"

Max was silent.

"Hoover?"

Max knew the voice. "Fitzgerald."

"You've got something of ours," Colonel Fitzgerald said. "We want it."

"I want to see Timms," said Hoover.

"There's no reason to involve the general in this. It's a straight trade. Your movie for ours."

"I want to see Timms," Max repeated. "No Timms, no deal, no movie. Understand?"

Fitzgerald leaned on him a little harder. "What you got today was a copy, and there's a lot more of them. We'll do whatever is necessary, Hoover, to get your cooperation. Right now, it's our little secret . . ."

"I guess you didn't hear me. No Timms, no deal."

Hoover heard a deep sigh come down the line. "All right," he said, as if giving into the petulant demands of an infant. "Ten o'clock tomorrow at the military airfield in Santa Monica. We'll have someone there to meet you."

"Good."

"You bring everything, we bring everything. Originals plus all the copies," said Fitzgerald. "Don't think of getting cute and keeping one back as some kind of insurance scheme."

Hoover did not answer. He hung up.

* * *

The rest of the night was spent in the basement as he ran the Timms film again and again, stopping the movie projector at the moment when Allison came onto the screen. It was the dark, haunted faces in the white and sterile room that concerned him. What were they? And how did it happen that they were on this little piece of film.

The final time he watched, he let the film run to the end, transfixed at Allison's sultry beauty and the wonder of her climax. As the film played out, a single clear memory crowded into his mind, a recollection so distinct he could have been watching a film of that, too.

It was the last night they had been together, the last time he had seen her alive. They met at the Mulholland Falls, she in her car, he in his. They stood side by side in front of the cars, smoking, not speaking. Lights glittered below and the wind blew gently, pine-scented and warm on their faces.

The whole of their lives had been forced into less than six months. They could barely remember the intense excitement of their meeting, the giddy happiness of their sixty-minute courtship, the electric intensity of their first sexual explorations, then the happy contentment of middle age, those few weeks, when they talked and laughed and could take time for dinner or a drink before they fell on one another. Then came the inevitable decline as guilt and more logistics began to intrude on the idyll arguments and tears and all those "I don't knows . . ."

Until this moment. They were at the end, and Allison knew it. She threw her cigarette to the dirt and ground it out.

"This is where you bring people to get rid of them, isn't it," she asked. There was anger in her voice.

For a moment he thought she was referring to his more unorthodox use of the Falls.

"It's over, right?"

Hoover shrugged. "It's not like that Allison . . . It's not just over . . . The thing is, you think you can make it work, you think you can have it both ways, but I can't. I'm sorry."

With a short, curt shake of her head she rejected his explanation and his apology. "No, Max," she said. "That's not it. We've got different problems. I never wanted it both ways . . ." She leaned over and kissed him on the cheek and then, without a look back, she walked to her car.

He stayed, watching the headlights of the car as she wound down to the plain. He could feel the place on his cheek where her lips had touched, like a burn.

* * *

At dawn he went to the bedroom. Katherine was sprawled, fully clothed, on the bed, an ashtray filled with Pall Malls on the bedside table. Her face was in shadow, and he assumed she was alseep. As quietly as he could, Hoover, walked to the dresser and removed a small snub-nosed revolver from the top drawer and buckled the holster to his ankle.

As he knelt, he heard the distinctive sound of a Zippo lighter clicking open. The flame flared, and a fresh cloud of blue smoke blew across the room.

"'I thought you were sleeping," said Max.

"I wasn't."

"What are you doing?"

He could hear the sheets rustle as she shrugged. "Thinking . . ."

He stood up and hesitated a moment, aware that she was watching him closely, as if she did not know him and was curious as to his identity. Hoover could feel the weight of the inspection, and it made him uneasy.

"What were you thinking about?" he asked.

Her reply was a short bitter laugh.

"I know what you're thinking," Hoover said. "But I don't know what you're thinking about it."

Katherine took a long pull on her cigarette.

"I'm not sure you'd want to know. It isn't good."

"You want me to leave for a while."

"At the very least," she said, turning away.

In the half-light of dawn, Hoover could see a figure leaning against the Buick parked in the driveway. Ellery Coolidge stepped forward the moment the front door of the house opened.

"Ellery, what are you doing here?" He glanced at his watch.

"We've got a problem, Max."

"We've had 'em before, Ellery."

"Not like this one, Max."

Hoover noticed that Coolidge was, for once, not eating anything. "This must be really bad, Ellery."

Coolidge nodded vigorously. "Max, Hoover—the other Hoover—called the chief from Washington, three o'clock this morning. The chief's been trying to get you ever since.

"Really?" said Hoover blandly. He opened the trunk of the car and put his briefcase inside. "What about?"

"Kidnap, assault, attempted murder . . . How's that for a start, Max?"

"You can tell the chief to tell Mr. Hoover that if I'd attempted to murder Special Agent McCafferty, Special Agent McCafferty would be dead." He slammed down the trunk lid and walked to the driver's side door.

"This is serious, Max. He's pissed—"

Hoover slid behind the wheel. "Not as pissed as he's going to be."

Coolidge ran around the prow of the car and got in on the passenger side. "Max, listen to me . . ."

"What are you doing, Ellery?"

"Wherever you're going, I'm coming, too," he said. "I'm not going back there and tell the chief you wouldn't come."

Hoover turned the key and fired up the big engine. "You know, Eddie Hall is right. This psychiatrist you're going to, he's turning you into nothing more than a piano teacher."

"She, Max," Coolidge corrected him. "She. It's a woman . . ."

22

Hoover and Coolidge walked across the tarmac at the Santa Monica Military Airfield, making for the DC-3 parked there, an elaborate military seal on the nose, tail, fuselage, and wings.

"This is going to turn bad, isn't it, Max?" said Coolidge.

Hoover nodded. "Yeah, I think so. . . . Listen, Ellery. You don't have to come. This is personal."

But Coolidge was stoic. "No. I'm coming."

"But this is something that I have to do, you don't. Why get mixed up in it? It's not your fight."

"No, Max," said Coolidge with a shake of his head. "We're partners. I'm coming."

The pilot poked his head out of the rear door of the trim little airliner. "Lieutenant Hoover?"

"I'm Hoover."

The pilot looked at Coolidge. "They told me that there was only going to be one passenger."

"Well, there's two."

"No skin off my ass," said the pilot. "There's plenty of room."

When the DC-3 taxied to a halt on the hardstand at the Atomic Research Center, an MP opened the doors and hustled Coolidge and Hoover out of the airplane as if they were criminals. Hoover's old friend, Fitzgerald's adjutant, the captain was there to meet them.

"We expected only one visitor on this flight, Hoover," the captain said. "That was the agreement."

"Sergeant Coolidge goes where I go."

The captain shrugged. "Suit yourself." He turned to the military policeman. "Sergeant, search them for weapons and escort them to Colonel Fitzgerald's office. I'll meet you there." He strode away hurrying, as if trying to get away from a bad smell.

The MP noncom removed their shoulder weapons and made a cursory search of Hoover's briefcase before escorting them to a staff car. Deviating from the normal seating arrangement,

Ellery Coolidge sat up front with the driver, Hoover sitting behind in the backseat with the MP.

As they drove through the base, Hoover gazed out the window, realizing that things were beginning to look familiar, buildings and landscapes that he had seen before—on film. He pointed to the low sleek building.

"What's that?" Hoover asked.

"That's a restricted area, sir," the noncom replied.

"Restricted?"

"Yes, sir."

"Can I see it?" Hoover asked, as if he hadn't heard the man.

"I'm sorry, sir," the MP repeated. "It's restricted. I'm not allowed to take you in there."

"Oh," said Hoover, "it's *restricted.*" Then, with sudden speed, Hoover reached into his back pocket and knocked out the sergeant with his sap. The man slumped in his seat.

Hoover grabbed the man's .45 and jammed it into the neck of the driver. "Stop the car." The driver stepped on the brake, and the car stopped abruptly. "Ellery, take the car and stash it. I'll meet you later. Here's the gun."

"Where you going?"

He pointed to the building he had seen on the film. "I'm going in there."

Hoover slipped out of the car and walked quickly across the burning asphalt toward the hospital. The building was not guarded, and it seemed deserted. He stood in the entrance area unsure of what to do next. Then, from down the hall, he heard a single anguished cry.

As he walked down the hall he heard a louder, longer more tortured scream. Pushing through the crash doors, Hoover found himself walking straight into the scene in the movie.

Hoover was standing in the large, sterile ward, the air heavy with the stinging smell of disinfectant. Everything in the room—the walls, the sheets, the beds—was painted an antiseptic hospital white. Everything in the room was white—except the patients. Black, Indian, Mexican, they lay inert in their beds, a tangle of tubes and drip feeders snaking across beds and into collapsing veins. Their jaws were slack and their mouths were open, fat tongues lolling. Many of the patients had hideous scarring, as if they had been scalded, livid red lesions, protuberant oozing growths on their faces and hands. More than one of them was dead. A woman stretched in a bed saw Hoover and managed to summon the strength to reach for him, groaning as she did so.

Max went to her bed and read the chart hanging at the foot of it. He moved to another bed, another chart. There were a lot of medical terms he did not know, but he knew enough to know what was wrong with these wretched people.

Coolidge pushed into the room. "Hey Max," he said. "I ditched the car . . ." He stopped and looked around. "What's going in?" His eyes went from bed to bed. "What's the matter with these people?"

"They've all got cancer," said Hoover. He took one last looked around the room at the sickening site. "Let's go, Ellery."

The front door of Timms's house was locked, and the dwelling appeared to be uninhabited. There was an eerie stillness about the place, and it did not seem a good idea to shoot their way into the house—the sound of the shot would carry a mile and bring Fitzgerald and the captain running with a hefty contingent of soldiers. Hoover knew he would be apprehended eventually, but he could not allow that to happen just at the moment.

"Ellery," said Hoover urgently. "I want you to stay here and cover the front of the house."

"You okay, Max?" asked Coolidge. "You sure you don't want me to come with you?"

"I'm fine. Don't worry," said Hoover, disappearing around the side of the house.

General Timms was on the balcony asleep. At first Timms appeared to be sleeping normally, but as Hoover moved closer he could see that the general was paler than he remembered him, gaunt, the skin of his cheeks sagging off the bone. His breath came in short labored gasps. The bed was not a normal piece of deck furniture, but a fancy electric hospital bed, the table next to it loaded with medicines, as well as a crystal pitcher of water and a glass in a sterile rap.

Hoover lowered the gun until it was next to the general's temple. He cocked the weapon, the metal grating with a sharp, loud rasp. Timms's eyes fluttered open, apparently unfazed by the weapon or his unexpected visitor.

"Lieutenant Hoover," he said with a slight, diffident smile. "I thought you were due to see Colonel Fitzgerald this afternoon."

Hoover nodded. "I am," he said. "I'll be seeing him later."

Timms's frail body was wracked with coughs, deep tearing coughs. He put his thin hand to his mouth and pointed at the pitcher of water with the other. Hoover broke the sterile bag, poured some of the water into the beaker, and held the rim of the glass to Timms's thin, pale lips. Hoover held back the man's head to allow the water to flow down his throat. Timms's hair was thin and coarse, the feeling of his skin dry and papery. The water seemed to help, and he revived a little when the coughing fit had blown itself.

"Thank you," the general gasped as he lay back on the pillows.

"What is it?" Hoover asked. "What has happened to you. Cancer?"

"Cancer," said Timms matter-of-factly. He grimaced as pain washed through his wasted body.

"Cancer . . . It's in my blood, my bones, even, they tell me now, in my brain . . ." He turned his unseeing eyes to Hoover. "I see a black hole when I look in the middle of your face, Lieutenant."

"I did not know that," said Hoover.

"I'll bet you've never seen a man with terminal cancer before, have you, Lieutenant?" Just as at their last meeting, it seemed that the general had a compulsion to educate him.

"You're wrong, General," Hoover replied. "I've seen a lot of people with terminal cancer. I've seen some worse off than you are right now. In fact, I saw a whole room full of terminal cancer on my way over here."

Timms smiled, as he remembered an old, treasured memory. "A hundred die so a thousand may live."

"Wait," said Hoover. "Those people in there, they were experiments? They didn't get it by accident?"

"Think of them as soldiers," said Timms.

Now it was all coming clear to Max. "They didn't look like soldiers to me. I'll bet they didn't look like soldiers to Allison, either . . . They looked like what they were, poor Negroes, Indians, Mexicans, the kind of people that big important men like you consider expendable." He smiled and shook his head wearily. "Allison, she always had a soft spot for the underdog. Jimmy Fields, me . . ."

"Me," said Timms.

"Don't kid yourself."

"I think she took pity on me to a degree . . . A lovely, vibrant girl like that and a man like me? Hardly a likely scenario."

"Did she know about your illness. Is that it? I assume you've been sick for a long time. This sort of thing doesn't happen overnight."

Timms shook his head. "With the amount of radiation I've been exposed to over my life, Lieutenant, when the cancer finally comes it spreads quickly." He paused a moment. "But no, hers was a different kind of pity. But it amounts to the same thing . . . Those people are dying, and I might be in a more comfortable bed, but I'm dying, too."

"They didn't volunteer for this duty," said Hoover angrily. "The system took care of you pretty good while you we're healthy. Those people never got anything; Allison never got anything but killed."

"Why would I kill her?" Timms asked. "She showed me pleasures I never dreamed of. It's almost all I think about these days. I'm sure you understand that. She was spectacular! Wasn't she, Hoover?"

"Yeah," said Hoover. "She was something."

"Her death . . . It was a mistake."

"What do you mean?" said Hoover angrily. "A mistake? A mistake is when you add figures up wrong on your slide rule, General. Allison's death was not a mistake."

"An error of judgment, then," Timms conceded. "An overzealous reaction to a perceived threat to national security."

Hoover nodded. "She saw the cancer ward. And took the pictures."

Timms appeared to have exhausted his small store of strength. He closed his eyes, and his voice faded like someone turning down the volume on a radio.

"A word of advice, Lieutenant . . . Let it go . . ." Hoover thought he had drifted off, but not quite. "The world is a dangerous place . . ."

Hoover watched the general, then opened his briefcase and took out the tin of film, placing it on the table next to the pitcher of water.

Timms was still aware that he was there. "What is that?"

Hoover popped open the can and showed the film to Timms, not sure if he could see it or not. "It's the film," he said. "The film of the ward and the one with you and Allison Pond."

Timms smiled and nodded. "You're much more intelligent than you seem, you know. That must be an advantage in your field. In mine, everyone is so desperate to seem so much more clever than they really are. That can be something of a drawback in atomic science . . ."

"I don't want to think about that . . ."

"Isn't it ironic? The thing I helped create is killing me. You figured out the first part of the film, didn't you? How did you know?"

"I didn't," said Hoover. "I guessed. I couldn't see Allison being killed for something like sex."

Timms smiled, his voice ironic. "Not at the government level, no. Sex is too insignificant in a place like this."

The sliding door leading to the balcony slipped open, and Fitzgerald, the captain, and a squad of soldiers emerged. Hanging back were a couple of more soldiers boxing in Coolidge.

"What now, Colonel Fitzgerald?" Timms asked.

"Sir, they've breached security," Fitzgerald announced for the benefit of the soldiers. "This man came here to harm you."

One of the soldiers relieved Hoover of his .45.

"But they've brought me a film," said Timms mildly.

"Pardon me, General," said Fitzgerald. "But they have compromised top secret scientific areas. We have a test scheduled in one hour."

"I understand that perfectly, Colonel," said General Timms. "Now, perhaps you could see to it that these men are transported back to Los Angeles."

Fitzgerald seemed to be fighting with his anger. "With all due respect, the security of this particular installation is my priority, General Timms. I'm afraid I cannot allow this to happen."

General Timms forced as much steel into his voice as he could muster. "Colonel Fitzgerald, these men are not my enemies. Take them back."

Fitzgerald teetered on the edge of the decision, apparently unsure of which way to go. Finally, his shoulders slumped, and he seemed to surrender to the great authority of the general's two stars.

"All right," he said, picking up the canister of film. Hoover watched him closely.

"All right, *sir*!" Timms snapped.

23

The plane that had carried them to the test site was not the plane that was going to take them back to Los Angeles. The other one had been festooned with government seals, the second carried to markings of any kind: no seals, no insignia, no army tag, no FAA registration.

It was then that Hoover realized that they were being sent to the army equivalent of Mulholland Falls. He turned to Fitzgerald and looked at him hard. "I don't suppose we could have our guns back."

"Of course," said the colonel. "They will be returned to you the instant you touch down in Los Angeles. I'll do it personally."

"Personally?"

"The captain and I have business in Los

Angeles,'' Fitzgerald said lightly, as if they were the best of friends, having resolved some silly misunderstanding. ''We're going to catch a ride down with you, if that's all right with you.''

Hoover almost smiled, truly amused by the colonel's unbelievable gall. ''It's your plane, Colonel,'' said Hoover. ''Sit anywhere you like.''

''Thank you, Lieutenant.'' The two officers came aboard and settled in their seats. The pilot gunned the engines, and the plane moved off, taxiing to the head of the runway. The plane turned into the wind and seemed to pause for a moment, as if preparing itself for the ordeal of takeoff.

The engines roared and the aircraft accelerated, lifting lightly off the ground, climbing sharply for cruising altitude. As the plane soared into the sky, the temperature inside the can dropped quickly, and soon it was cold—much colder than on the trip from the city to the desert. Coolidge looked around, searching for the source of the frigid air, and when he found it, his jaw dropped.

''Max, there's no door on this plane,'' he turned from the door and gaped at Hoover. ''Why is the door missing?''

Hoover looked over his shoulder at the open space, then back at Coolidge. ''It's simple, Ellery, they're going to throw us out of the airplane. I told you that you shouldn't come along."

Ellery was having trouble making sense of his words. "They're going to throw us from the plane?" he said incredulously.

"That's right. Just like they threw out Allison Pond."

The words seemed to hit Ellery like a flurry of punches. He slumped in his seat, as if someone had beaten the air out of him, shaking his head. The roar of the engines drowned out his whispers, but he was saying over and over again: *they threw her out of the plane* . . .

Fitzgerald and his aide had their guns out now, and they were aimed squarely at Hoover. It was obvious that they didn't consider Ellery Coolidge much of a threat. Get rid of Hoover first and deal with the other one at your leisure.

"You gave us the wrong film, Lieutenant Hoover." Colonel Fitzgerald actually looked disappointed. "You should have known that I wouldn't be much interested in a police-training film about clap. That would have been of much more interest to the general. He was uncommonly interested in sex, but he never seemed to consider the hazards along with the pleasures . . . . Sort of like you, Hoover. And with the same woman, too. It's amazing what sex with the right chippy will make even responsible men stoop to. And to do it on film, too . . ."

Hoover knew that Fitzgerald was trying to provoke him into an attack so he could shoot and make two murders all nice and legal. But Hoover refused to be drawn.

"You didn't abide by the rules," said Fitzgerald. "You were supposed to give us everything you have for everything we have. That was the understanding."

"I appreciate that, Colonel," said Hoover. "But you see, there's a problem. One you didn't foresee."

"And what would that be?"

"You sent the film you had to my house . . ."

Fitzgerald merely shrugged. "We needed to get your attention, Hoover. Can you think of a better way? Besides, no copies were sent to the newspapers or to members of the Los Angeles Police Department—"

Hoover felt his self-control fraying, and he cut off Fitzgerald. "You sent the film to my house, Colonel. You addressed it to my wife . . . and she watched it."

Fitzgerald started to speak, but Hoover held up his hand to stop him. "The problem is, I don't care now who sees it. You see what I mean? I don't have anything to lose."

The plane began to bank, a long, slow dip to

one side, the desert below appearing through the cabin windows. The captain stood up, steadying himself with a hand pressed against the low ceiling of the plane.

Coolidge seemed to have pulled out of his stupor a bit. He looked from the captain to Fitzgerald and then to the open door.

"Tell me, Fitzgerald, does Timms know about this?"

"The general is ill," said Fitzgerald dismissively. "He requires a great deal of medical care."

"Who decided to throw Allison out of the plane?"

Fitzgerald smirked. "If such a thing had happened, the general would not have been informed.

"Timms would not have made that decision?"

"Of course not."

"It would have been you? You were the one who decided to kill her," said Hoover.

"That's right . . . If he couldn't intervene on her behalf, he cannot intervene to save you . . . No one can intervene here." Fitzgerald smiled. "The good General Timms will go to his grave believing that you are alive and well and serving the public good in Los Angeles."

"Well, I'm glad he'll die happy," said Hoover. "But I wanted to know the truth about Allison."

Anger had built up in Coolidge, a slow boil at first, but now he felt like he was full of scalding steam. He looked at Fitzgerald, he looked at the open door. For a split second he could imagine Allison's terrifying last moments, a horrible death brought about by these unfeeling men.

"They threw her out of the plane!" said Coolidge.

There was rage in Coolidge's voice. The captain and Fitzgerald had overlooked this threat; they swung their guns to cover him. Coolidge looked to Max, then turned to face the two military officers.

"*They threw her out of a plane!*" he shouted.

Coolidge suddenly erupted from his seat, throwing his considerable form straight at the captain. There were two shots, Coolidge took them both, but they could not slow him down, and he slammed into them like a bulldozer. Ellery Coolidge screamed as his big hands closed around the captain's throat and shook him, smacking his head against the steel floor of the plane. Coolidge's eyes were glazed with rage, and he seemed to be in some sort of trance. Without thinking, Coolidge bared his teeth and sunk them into the fleshy ball of the captain's cheek. His tortured screams mixed with Coolidge's bearlike growl.

The moment Coolidge jumped, Hoover had

left his seat, diving for Fitzgerald, grabbing his gun hand and jamming it straight up. The big gun roared six times, the slugs puncturing the skin of the aircraft. Fitzgerald clawed at Hoover's face, his nails raking his face.

The plane was rolling crazily, and the four men tumbled. The gun came out of Fitzgerald's hand and clattered away.

Coolidge roared and stood up, picking up the captain and held him over his head like a professional wrestler, body slamming him into the ceiling, then throwing him hard to the floor, the captain's right arm twisted under him. The crack of shattering bone was as loud as a rifle shot.

Ellery fell on the pain-wracked man and snapped his head from side to side, bludgeoning his skull against anything hard he could find. The man's face vanished in seconds, replaced by the raw pulpy mass of blood, flesh, and bone fragments. There was a chance that he could have been dead before Coolidge threw him out the open door.

Ellery Coolidge's great strength drained from him, and he slumped against the wall of the plane. His eyes were glassy, and his breathing was rapid and shallow. His face was white and mottled like old ivory.

Hoover and Fitzgerald were more evenly matched in strength, but Hoover had the extra stimulus of rage. He pounded his fist into Fitzgerald's face again and again, oblivious to the pain of the split skin and bruised bones of his right hand. One final blow and Fitzgerald toppled. As he fell, Hoover pounced on the big .45 and aimed it straight at Fitzgerald's head.

"You're right, Colonel," said Hoover. "No one can intervene here. You're a dead man."

Fitzgerald looked at him through bleeding eyes, and he spoke with torn and bloody lips. "You're pathetic, Hoover," Fitzgerald spat. "You let emotion get in the way of your job." He pounded his chest, leaving bloody prints on his once faultless uniform. "Me, I did my job. She died because she was in our way."

"She died for nothing!" Hoover tossed the gun aside and grabbed Fitzgerald by the shirt. For an instant Hoover saw wild fear in the colonel's eyes and then he was gone, tumbling end over end earthward.

Hoover staggered away from the opening and sunk down next to Coolidge. Ellery managed a weak smile.

The plane banked sharply. Hoover and Coolidge somersaulted, their arms and legs tangling.

"What the hell is going on?" Hoover yelled. He looked toward the flight deck and saw that the cockpit door had been pierced by a handful of slugs from the guns. Hoover scrambled to his feet the threw open the door to the cockpit. The pilot was slumped over the controls, a large red stain spreading on the back of his shirt.

Hoover pulled the pilot from the joystick, and he slumped back in the seat, the controls rolling back with him, the nose of the DC-3 lurching upward suddenly. Coolidge had managed to stumble into the cramped room.

"Is he dead?"

The pilot moaned, and his eyelids trembled. "No," said Hoover. "He's still alive." Max slapped the pilot a half a dozen times. "Hey, wake up! Come on! We need you to fly this plane."

Coolidge's newfound sensitivity seemed to re-assert itself. "It's okay," he yelled in the pilot's ear. "You're okay."

The pilot opened his eyes and looked around groggily. "Where are we?"

Hoover glanced out the window. "We're in the mountains." The man took a deep breath, wincing in pain as he did so. But the agony seemed to clear his foggy brain. He peered out of the front windscreen and managed to get a look at some of the larger instruments.

"All right. Keep my hands on the stick," the pilot said. He throttled back, and the plane steadied.

"He's okay!" Coolidge yelled. "We're going to be okay, Max!"

The plane was level and stable, and they flew straight for several minutes. Hoover let out a great rush of air, and allowed himself to relax a notch, slumping into the empty seat of the co-pilot. Then the pilot's eyes turned up in his head, and he slumped to one side.

"Jesus Christ!" Hoover shouted. "Don't go, wake up."

Coolidge's more aggressive side came back in a hurry. He slapped the man hard. "Wake up and fly this plane, or I'll kill you right here."

"We gotta land this plane now," said Hoover. "This guy is going to die before we get to an airport."

"Can you land this plane?" Coolidge demanded.

"I don't know," said the pilot. "Is there any flat ground?"

Hoover threw himself against the window and studied the terrain below. It was hard to tell from that height what was flat and what was not. If they didn't get down, they were going to die anyway—Hoover chose a piece of desert at random and prayed that it was flat.

"Yeah," he said. "Right up ahead, over that ridge."

The plane lost altitude at an alarming rate.

They also seemed to be slowing down. But neither Coolidge nor Hoover seemed to notice that. Both men were preoccupied with something else.

"What about the wheels?" Hoover yelled. "Shouldn't we be putting the wheels down?"

"We don't need 'em."

Coolidge shook the pilot roughly. "What do you mean we don't need the wheels? Are you trying to kill us, you, you son of a bitch."

"No, no," said the pilot. "It's safer without them."

Sweat was pouring from Coolidge's forehead. "What do you mean? Even I know you can't land a plane without the wheels down!"

"We're gonna belly-land," said the pilot. "Don't worry. I've done this before. It's gonna be okay."

The plane descended, the desert becoming more and more distinct. The tension in the cabin shot up like mercury in a thermometer on a hot day. The pilot hit two switches, and for a moment the air was full of the smell of gasoline until the rushing wind carried it away.

"What the hell was that?" screamed Coolidge.

"I dumped the gas," said the pilot.

"You did *what*!"

"So we don't explode on impact . . . Where's

my airspeed?'' The pilot was blinking his eyes, trying to focus them on the jiggling needles in the instrument housings. "I can't see clearly."

"Where is it?" Hoover looked closely at the panel. "This one? It says one fifty, one forty . . . one twenty . . . one hundred . . . ninety . . ."

"Okay," the pilot gasped. "That's enough." The front of his shirt was soaked with blood, as the cloth soaked up the gore from the back wound like a piece of saturated blotting paper.

"Hold on," wheezed the pilot. "It's going to be okay." His eyes closed and his face seemed to shut flat, like a venetian blind, his features slack.

The ground rushed up to meet them, and there was a spine-juddering thump as the full weight of the plane collided with the earth. The aircraft plowed through the sand, throwing up a great V of earth like the bow of a powerboat slicing through water. The banshee wail of metal on stone was so loud it blotted out all other sound, the cabin filled with a hot, acrid electric smell as systems shorted out and shut down. The tip of one of the misshapen propeller blades caught on some rocks, and the plane spun around, a hard sharp turn to the right.

Then all was silent. For a moment Hoover couldn't move, couldn't decide if he was dead or alive. In his mind he tossed a coin, and it came down alive.

"Ellery," he said softly. "That's it. We're on the ground." Hoover extricated himself from his seat and turned to the pilot. There was no pulse, and Hoover felt a flash of sorrow.

Coolidge needed to lean hard on Hoover to stagger out of the broken fuselage of the plane. They tottered as far away as they could on their shaky legs and then collapsed to the hot earth.

Coolidge smiled at Hoover, a dazed look in his eyes, his voice oddly controlled and light. "Are you okay, Max?"

"Sure, Sure, Ellery. How about you?"

Ellery shivered. "Fine. I'm a little cold, that's all."

Hoover laughed and fell back on the burning sand. "Ellery, how can you be cold. We're in the middle of the desert."

A crooked smile crossed Ellery Coolidge's face. "Yeah. Funny ain't it?" he thought for a moment. "You know what, Max, I think I'll just sit here and think about that for a while." The smile vanished as if someone had thrown a switch and turned it off.

"Ellery? Ellery?" said Hoover scurrying across the ground like a sand crab. "You okay?"

Coolidge's eyes were unfocused, and he did his best to smile. Hoover pulled open his suit coat and found that Coolidge's normally snowy white shirt was sodden with dark blood. Coolidge looked with interest, but no special concern at his own blood.

"Hey, Max, I got shot," he said. He slumped sideways, but his eyes remained open. "Max, my psychiatrist isn't going to like this . . . You know, while it was all happening, I felt good again . . . It was like the old days; it was like it used to be."

"Ellery, don't talk. Please."

"I like to talk, Max," said Coolidge. But his voice was slow and deep, like a record winding down. "It's good to get it out . . . Max?" Coolidge sighed sadly. "Tell me the truth . . . is there something wrong with me? Wrong in the head I mean?"

"Ellery," said Hoover, his throat suddenly very dry. "Whatever you are, you are the best at it. The best there is . . ."

He knew that Ellery was going fast. When the big man looked up at Max, Hoover could see that his eyes were heavy with the onset of death.

"Hey . . . do you mean that?"

"Yeah," said Hoover, his voice hoarse. "We're partners, right? Partners don't lie to partners."

Coolidge smiled and nodded. With a serene, calm look of contentment, Coolidge slipped away, a remarkably peaceful end for a man who had been angry most of his life. Hoover hadn't burst into tears since childhood until now. He had seen many people die over the years, and many of those deaths had saddened and depressed him. But not one had affected him like this. For a moment the hardened, world-weary Max Hoover vanished, the fierceness of the hard-case tough guy was stripped away in an instant.

Hoover put his head down on the bloody chest of his dead friend and cried for them both . . .

Suddenly, there was a flash of light on the horizon. A sheet of light so bright it changed the desert sky from day to night. A mushroom cloud rose from the desert floor. As Hoover held on to Coolidge's lifeless body, the wind and the dust whipped around them, as if trying to tear them apart.

EPILOGUE

The Los Angeles Police Department gave Ellery Coolidge a real nice send-off. There was an honor guard, a band of bagpipers, a nice bronze coffin (not the best, but respectable, paid for by the Detective's Benevolent Association), a flag on it like bacon on BLT, and a lot of mourners.

It was the second cop funeral in ten days, but that didn't stop the hundreds of people connected with the department, not to mention a lot of restaurant owners and bartenders coming out to pay their respects to Sergeant Ellery Coolidge. In truth, Coolidge drew a bigger crowd than poor dumb Earl the week before—although the two funerals had some things in common. The chief was there, of course, and the mayor, and most of the city council. Earl and Ellery got the same coffin and more or less the same eulogy (dedicated officer, fearless in the face of danger, devoted to public service, gave his life without a thought, etc. etc.)

Coolidge had been a Catholic once upon a time (though not recently), and the service at graveside lasted a little longer than Protestant funerals. By the time the priest got to the end of the rite, the mayor had one leg in his limousine and the chief had looked at his watch two or three more times than was strictly appropriate.

Hoover didn't care. The lengthy ceremony gave Hoover ample time to look over the graveside at his ex-wife. He looked at Katherine with a profound love in his heart, but a love that he could keep hidden.

They had not spoken since that early morning when he had left for Nevada a few days before. He had not even expected her to show up at Coolidge's funeral—not because she did not love and respect his old comrade in arms, but because he doubted that she would want to run into the husband who had betrayed her so. Max could not help but feel proud, though, that she had come, regardless of the pain, to pay her respects to a good man who she knew lived and worked among the evil.

Eventually, the priest finished with his prayers. All the platitudes that were going to be aired had been said. The pipers had played "Amazing Grace," the bugler had blown "Taps," the honor guards of LAPD marksmen had fired their blanks into the summer air, the flag bearer had folded the Stars and Stripes into a neat, sharp triangle and presented it to Coolidge's tearful, drably dressed mother . . .

Then Hoover, Hall, and Relyea stepped forward from the crowd of mourners. The three men did not speak; they did not cry; they merely looked at the coffin. Then Hoover placed Ellery Coolidge's fedora on the lid as if conferring a decoration. The three men stood at the edge of the grave and watched as their comrade and friend was lowered slowly into the ground.

The three men didn't stay around for any more of the obsequies, walking back to the car, sharing a moment of silence as they lit their cigarettes, watching the crowd around Ellery's grave, and listening to the priest finish up. As the mourners began to stream away, Hoover searched with his eyes among the people until he found Katherine. He detached himself from the group, walked to her, and fell in step next to her.

"I hear they broke up the squad," said Katherine.

"That's right," said Hoover nodding. "There's no squad without Ellery."

"What are you going to do?"

Hoover gave her a slow smile. "Oh . . . I don't know . . . I honestly don't know, Kay."

They walked among the tombstones, silent for a moment. Then she stopped and faced him square on.

"Tell me, did you ever think about leaving me for her?"

Hoover did not hesitate with his answer. "No . . . Kay, no."

"Why did you stop seeing her?" she asked.

His answer came from the heart. "Kay, I love you. I've always loved you. And I didn't want that between us. When I realized the mistake I made, I didn't want that between us, either." He shrugged and looked sad. "But it's there, between us. I guess it always will be . . ."

"It's never going to be the same, Max."

"Yeah, I know . . ."

"Max, I love you. You see, I gave my heart once in my life, and I gave it to you. Nothing will ever change that."

Max Hoover looked into her eyes. "Kay? Are you saying that you'll take me back?"

"Only if you promise me something . . ."

Hoover anticipated her request. "I promise, Kay. It will never happen again."

Katherine smiled. "I already know that, Max. I want you to promise me that you won't come home drunk and walk through the flowers again.''

She put her arms around his neck and kissed him deeply. Then she took his arm firmly in hers, and they walked out of the cemetery.

A few weeks later Coolidge's grave would be crowned with a fine tombstone, paid for by Max Hoover, Eddie Hall, and Arthur Relyea. It would be a nice piece of New Hampshire granite, but in Hoover's mind his marriage to Katherine would be the true monument to Ellery Coolidge.